The Harbinger of Forgotten Things

Anuci Press

Tanuci69@gmail.com

First paperback edition 2024

Anuci Press edition 2024

www.anuci-press.com

Cover Design by Adrian Medina

https://fabledbeastdesign.wordpress.com

ISBN 979-8-9914345-7-7 (paperback)

ISBN 979-8-9914345-8-4(eBook)

Contents

THE NIGHT MOM DIED

Thirteen-year-old Cecil Harbinger had always believed in magic. Like when he opened the fridge one day before breakfast and discovered he still had a yogurt left—he thought he finished it the previous day. Or like while snow blanketed the ground. Something picturesque existed about a winter wonderland despite the frigid air stinging his lungs during the colder months of the year. Or like when he was younger and had an imaginary scarecrow best friend. Scarecrow (as Cecil called him) existed in more than just Cecil's mind. His imaginary friend followed Cecil wherever he went, and he could actually see and talk to Scarecrow even if nobody else could. Or even like while he currently sat across from his mother at the dining room table while they enjoyed beef stew for dinner. Somehow, Cecil and Mom would get through dinner. Even if the silence between him and Mom proved more awkward than that time he memorized a poem for a school assignment, only to forget the words when standing in front of his class. So, Cecil didn't want to speculate about what thoughts presently weighed on Mom's mind. If something bothered her, then she could share. Until then, Cecil would believe life was perfect.

Mom lifted her gaze off the plate. "I'm proud of you, dear."

Cecil gaped. "Come again?"

"Giving up your imaginary friend couldn't have been easy, so I wanted to give credit where credit is due."

Cecil's stomach knotted. It had been one year since he last saw Scarecrow, and Cecil wasn't sure how he should feel about how his imaginary friend no longer existed. In the beginning, time passed slowly—almost as if every second resembled an hour. But now living life proved effortless. Like someone erased all traces of Scarecrow.

"Thanks," Cecil finally said.

"I'm being serious. Not needing an imaginary friend shows tremendous growth and progress—I couldn't be more pleased if I tried."

Cecil's heart thumped louder and faster. Yet again Mom forgot about the whole reason for Scarecrow's existence. To cope with Dad dying. Losing a parent shouldn't have happened during childhood let alone when Cecil was only eight years old. However, Cecil couldn't change the past. Nobody could. And that meant Cecil needed to accept Dad's death—all the tears in the world couldn't bring back Dad. Nothing could. Also, Cecil wasn't sure he'd want to bring Dad back from the dead if such a spell existed. Like it or not, actions had consequences. And Cecil didn't want to complete what series of tumultuous events might happen if he resurrected Dad. Nothing good came from tampering with the natural order of things regardless of how cruel and unfair death seemed.

"Never thought I'd see the day when you're speechless," Mom continued.

"What do you want me to say?" Cecil asked.

"Whatever. It's not important."

"You mentioned Scarecrow, not me."

"Don't say his name!"

"Why? Are you afraid we'll burst into flames if we refer to him by name?"

Mom scowled. "Doesn't matter. We can't take that risk."

Cecil furrowed his eyebrows. "Since when are you superstitious?"

"I'm not!" Mom stammered.

"No offense, but it kinda sounds like you are. And that's ironic considering how you chastised Dad about being superstitious."

Mom pursed her lips. "What do you know about irony?"

"I know enough."

Mom sighed. "Encouraging your love of reading was wrong. Kids shouldn't spend their time devouring books—they should be playing outside in the dirt."

Cecil scoffed. "That's overrated."

Mom bit her lip. "There's no need to argue."

"Huh?" Cecil took another bite of his beef stew, and the meat's tender flavors electrified his taste buds. Nothing like sinking his teeth into a soft piece of meat. Scarecrow hadn't been Cecil's only joy when Dad died. Food comforted Cecil during the early days of his grief too. Nothing like a delicious warm meal to get through a difficult day.

Mom's elbows slid onto the table. "I should have supported you more after your father died, but I didn't. And that was wrong. Hopefully, you can accept my apology."

A lump lingered in Cecil's throat. Life once again presented him with a choice. Forgiveness seemed fair. Nobody was perfect, including Cedric. Yet pettiness tempted Cedric. People might think the apocalypse arrived with how Mom previously ranted and raved about how dangerous Cecil having an imaginary friend was. Like take the stereotypical concept of older people sometimes acting melodramatic and multiply that by one hundred, and that'd illustrate how unnerved Mom acted by Cecil having Scarecrow in his life.

Cecil coughed, clearing the nervousness from his throat. "Fine. I forgive you."

Mom's face lit up. "Really?"

"Yup. No sense in arguing over what already happened."

Mom's eyebrows knitted together. "When did you get so wise?"

Cecil shrugged. "Sometime after turning twelve."

"Good to know."

"I never meant to offend you by having an imaginary friend."

"Don't worry about it. Anyway, how about we change the topic?"

Cecil nodded. "Good idea."

"I was gonna wait a little longer before mentioning this, but I made apple pie for dessert."

Cecil smiled. "Sure you aren't trying to butter me up for something?"

"Not this time." Mom paused for a beat. "Besides, an occasional sweet won't kill us."

"Point taken. But don't tell the fun police that."

Mom let out a small laugh. "Agreed."

A warm sensation spread through Cecil's insides. He couldn't remember the last time Mom chuckled. Witnessing Mom's amusement needed to happen more often. Everyone deserved happiness every now and then. Therefore, Cecil wished this moment with Mom would last forever. He would've given almost anything to be able to take a picture of the current moment. No explanation necessary how life would get gloomy one day, and it'd be fun to be able to recall the present moment in concrete detail. But no. According to Mom, only rich people bought cameras—they were expensive.

Mom yawned. "I should get the apple pie."

"Why? Afraid you'll fall asleep if you don't fetch it now?"

"I'll be fine. Nothing a strong cup of coffee can't fix."

Cecil's eyes widened. "At this hour?"

"A lot of people like to have coffee after a meal."

"If you say so."

Mom wagged a finger. "Just remember I'm the adult, not you."

Cecil jabbed his fist through the air. "Darn."

"And the stew was okay?"

Cecil almost smacked his hand over his head. Mom worrying about dinner seemed futile. There were more complicated dishes to cook than stew. In fact, Cecil witnessed Mom cook the stew enough times that he could make the dish himself.

Cecil's grin expanded. "It was your best one yet."

"Good." Mom grabbed a napkin, then wiped a bit of broth from her upper lip.

"Can we have the apple pie now?"

"Sure thing, honey."

Cecil stretched his arms while Mom stood. From the corner of his eye, something caught his attention. More specifically, someone. He would've recognized the denim overalls and long-sleeve plaid shirt of the person who towered behind Mom anywhere.

"What are you doing here, Scarecrow?" Cecil asked.

"What?" Scarecrow demanded. "No 'hello' or 'happy to see me?'" I mean, come on, Cecil. I thought I meant more to you."

Mom grunted. "Why did you just mention your imaginary friend? I thought we moved beyond that? Don't tell me you lied to me?"

Cecil opened his mouth, yet words escaped him. Life always surprised Cecil regardless of how many books he read. The tightness in his throat only intensified since Scarecrow appeared moments earlier.

Cecil couldn't get over the moonlight trickling in from the dining room window, which glinted against the object in Scarecrow's hands. He just couldn't fathom why Scarecrow held an axe while standing behind Mom.

Mom pursed her lips. "You could at least say something, Cecil. I mean, you owe me that much."

Cecil maintained eye contact with Scarecrow. "What are you doing?"

Scarecrow expelled a gleeful cackle. "You were stolen from me, and someone needs to be punished."

"Scarecrow, no!" Cecil said, voice cracking.

Scarecrow pouted. "I've made my decision!"

Mom hissed. "For the last time, Scarecrow isn't real!"

"Does this seem real to you?" In one swift motion, Scarecrow swung his axe, decapitating Mom.

Cecil pressed his hand against his mouth, muffling screams. Mom's head thumped against the ground a few feet away from Cecil. Blood oozed everywhere like when a dam broke during a flood.

Mom couldn't be dead, yet she was. No amount of blinking changed how Mom's head lay on the floor in the distance.

Cecil yelled. Being an orphan before becoming a teenager happened in bedtime stories, not real life. And Cecil wanted nothing more than to punch a pillow. Losing one parent proved bad enough. However, Mom also dying seemed extra cruel. Almost as if the universe took pleasure in his misery. So, Cecil must've been the unluckiest kid in the world. Misfortune shouldn't strike twice, yet in Cecil's case it had.

Cecil couldn't understand what he did to deserve such a terrible fate, though. He wouldn't wish his current predicament on his worst enemy. Doing so would've been beyond cruel. And that wasn't something Cecil wanted to be a part of. Not now. Not ever. He hoped to be better than that. In theory, at least.

Tears wetted Cecil's eyes. No point in worrying about seeming weak. It was just him and Scarecrow, so nobody would ever know about Cecil's current outburst. Besides, his life couldn't get any worse. Therefore, Cecil might as well cry.

Cecil sobbed louder. "You didn't have to murder my mother!"

"Oh, but I did."

"What are you gonna do next? Kill me?"

"No. Not yet, anyway."

"Then what?""

"You'll find out soon enough."

Scarecrow vanished into thin air, then Cecil's breathing became more belabored with each passing second. He couldn't fathom Scarecrow becoming homicidal—the old Scarecrow hadn't even so much as raised his voice once. So, Cecil didn't want to speculate about what the following day would bring. It'd probably be nothing good. That much Cecil was certain of.

Help Me

Tree branches rattled in the wind while the moon shined from above in the cloudless sky. Cecil took several deep breaths while counting to ten in his head. Luckily for him, his BFF Aurora lived across the street. If there was ever a time when he'd ask for help, then his current predicament qualified. Contacting the authorities seemed futile. Cecil didn't have to be the smartest person in the world to realize what happened to Mom looked bad. Telling the sheriff that his former imaginary best friend killed Mom didn't quite roll off the tongue. Cecil couldn't prove what happened. So, chatting with Aurora was his best option. And maybe, just maybe, Aurora could help him fix his situation. He didn't have anything to lose—Mom couldn't die twice, after all.

Aurora also understood Cecil the best out of all his friends. They both experienced losses early in life. In Aurora's case, her mother died, not her father. But semantics didn't matter. Cecil and Aurora shared a pain nobody else in their seventh-grade class did.

Cecil rang the doorbell, then paced back and forth. In a perfect world, Cecil would ooze confidence. However, life was anything but perfect. And that meant Cecil needed to be realistic about what he was and wasn't capable of.

The door opened, revealing Aurora.

"What are you doing here?" she asked.

Cecil's jaw lowered. "Didn't know where else to go."

Aurora raised her eyebrows. "I see..."

"Can I come in, or what?"

Aurora gesticulated at Cecil, and he entered her home. The lock snicked. And if Mom's death didn't occupy his current thoughts, then Cecil would've commented about how Aurora locking the front door proved best. These days, people could never be too careful. Mom's death proved that truth. Safety had never once been an issue before for Cecil and Mom. Yet Mom died. And that was that.

Aurora huffed. "I can't help you unless you tell me what's wrong. I'm not trying to be mean. That's just a simple fact."

Cecil's breathing slowed down. When Aurora was right, she was right. He couldn't argue with her comment. But Cecil didn't know where to begin. Being best friends meant they told each other anything. However, Cecil couldn't bring himself to reveal his former imaginary best friend murdered Mom. Almost as if keeping the thought inside him meant Mom hadn't died. Denial always proved to be a powerful tool. And the current moment was no exception. The only question that remained was how far Cecil would go with the charade. Eventually, the truth always got out. Therefore, Cecil couldn't keep Mom's death a secret forever—doing so wouldn't be realistic.

Aurora threw a glance inside. "Why don't we go chat in the living room?"

"Good idea."

His stomach churned while he trailed after Aurora. The situation couldn't be more ridiculous if he tried. His best friend needed to know Mom died. No matter how much Cecil wished the opposite was true, he couldn't get around that fact.

The clock on the wall chimed, and Cecil winced. His current surroundings might as well have been spinning around him. No telling what might happen next in light of Mom's death. That was the way life would be for Cecil for the foreseeable. The sensation of constant dread would remain so long as Scarecrow could appear on a whim.

Aurora gave Cecil a pleading look. "Please tell me what's wrong..."

"Someone murdered my mother."

A chill rolled up Cecil's back while the comment lingered in his mind—Mom's death was official now that he spoke about it. And his pulse quickened. Half an hour later, Mom's death still sucked. And nothing anybody did or said changed how Mom died.

Aurora scratched the back of her head. "I don't understand..."

"Remember how I used to have an imaginary best friend?"

"Yeah. But what does Scarecrow have to do with your mother dying?"

Cecil flinched. "He beheaded my mother."

Aurora gasped. "What now?"

"I'm serious, Aurora. I wouldn't joke about something so serious. Hopefully, you know I'm not that type of person?"

"Relax. I believe you."

"But it's not like I can contact the authorities about Mom dying. I can't prove what happened actually happened. You get what I'm saying?"

"Why me?"

"Do you even have to ask?"

Aurora scrunched her eyebrows. "Did you seriously answer a question with another question?"

Cecil whimpered. "Please help me. I don't wanna get blamed for my mother's death."

"What's going on?" someone called out.

Cecil and Aurora tilted their heads at the same time. Aurora's father, Mr. Dexley, just entered the living room.

Aurora giggled. "I thought you were working in the basement?"

"I asked you a question!" Mr. Dexley rubbed his bushy mustache—which was more gray than black—then gave Cecil and Aurora a stern look. If Cecil wanted Aurora to help him, then they needed to get Mr. Dexley out of the living room ASAP. It didn't matter how nice Aurora's father behaved. Someone else knowing about Mom's death besides Aurora meant adding another variable to the situation. And Cecil couldn't have that.

Aurora wrapped a strand of hair around her finger. "Cecil and I felt like hanging out. Is that okay with you?"

The vein surfaced on Mr. Dexley's head. "Being older doesn't mean I'm clueless., You said something about your mother dying."

Cecil dug his nails into his palms. So much for Mr. Dexley not finding out about Mom dying. Having one thing go right would've been nice. Cecil wasn't asking for gold or a mansion. He just needed some semblance of a plan.

"Well?" Mr. Dexley demanded.

"It's complicated," Cecil mumbled.

Aurora placed her hands on her lap. "You can tell him the truth, Cecil. I mean, I know it won't be easy. But you can trust my dad. He's the last person who would judge anyone. Isn't that right, Dad?"

Mr. Dexley nodded. "Absolutely."

Cecil wiped his eyes—so much for the no crying thing. "I don't want you to think I'm crazy."

"I'd never think that," Mr. Dexley said.

Aurora nudged Cecil. "Have you forgotten who you're talking to?"

Cecil fought back laughter regardless of Aurora being right—he didn't have it in him to be amused about anything, whether small or big. Polite people ignored the whispers throughout Hicklewapper, yet Cecil could only feign ignorance for so long. By day, Mr. Dexley ran a pawn shop on Main Street, but by night he was an inventor/amateur scientist. And unfortunately for Mr. Dexley, he didn't have any scientific accomplishments or successful inventions to his name.

Not caring about Mr. Dexley being a laughing stock proved best, though. And not because accepting a BFF's quirky parent was the polite thing to do. It wasn't Cecil's place to judge Mr. Dexley. If the situation were reversed, he wouldn't want someone to judge him. Cecil had baggage even if he wasn't an inventor/amateur scientist. That was what life entailed when losing a parent at eight. Like it or not, time didn't heal all wounds. Not a day went by when Cecil didn't think about Dad.

"My former imaginary best friend killed my mother earlier this evening." Cecil's back ached, then he adjusted his posture on the couch. He should've known the couch was trouble from the first time he saw it. A plum-colored couch didn't inspire much confidence, and Cecil hoped Aurora hadn't suggested her parents get this particular couch. If that were the case, then Cecil didn't know Aurora as well as he thought he did. "And if you don't believe me, you can go to my house. You'll find both my mother's head detached a few feet away from her body in the dining room."

Mr. Dexley's Adam's apple throbbed. "That's terrible. I'm sorry to hear that."

Cecil fought back the tickle in his throat. "You aren't gonna scrutinize my story?"

Mr. Dexley averted his gaze. "Believe it or not, your mother dying isn't the first strange thing I've heard this week."

"And what's that supposed to mean?" Cecil asked.

Mr. Dexley grimaced. "Never you mind that."

Cecil let out a loud sob. "I can't be blamed for my mother's death!"

Mr. Dexley exhaled a deep breath. "Understood."

"What are we supposed to do, Dad?" Aurora asked.

Mr. Dexley stroked his chin. "I'm not sure."

Aurora rolled her eyes. "That's not helpful—no offense or anything."

"None taken," Mr. Dexley said.

"You get how the situation looks bad for Cecil, right?" Aurora asked.

Mr. Dexley cradled his hands behind his head. "Yeah, I get that."

"The worst part is I don't know when Scarecrow might strike again." Cecil looked away, focusing his attention on the gray carpet.

"Choosing a scarecrow as an imaginary best friend is an interesting choice," Mr. Dexley said. "Can't say that'd be my first choice for an imaginary friend."

Aurora gave her father a dirty look. "I thought you weren't gonna judge Cecil?"

Mr. Dexley bit his lip. "You're right. Sorry."

"Don't worry about it," Cecil whispered.

Aurora rose. "We can't let Cecil be blamed for his mother's death."

"We won't," Mr. Dexley said.

Aurora crossed her arms. "Then what's the plan?"

"Yeah, we can't just stand here chatting," Cecil said. "We need to do something."

Mr. Dexley exhaled a deep breath. "Unfortunately, we're gonna have to burry your mother's body in the woods behind your house—it's the easiest way to deal with the situation. I'll go get the shovels and tarp.

"Wonderful," Cecil said, somewhat sarcastically.

Mr. Dexley exited the living room. The shuffling of his footsteps grew fainter and fainter until the noise no longer echoed. Life sucked, but Cecil wasn't alone. So, he'd hold onto that. Aurora and her father didn't have to help Cecil. Yet they were. And for that, Cecil was more thankful than they could ever imagine. Their generosity was the only thing Cecil had, after all.

Burying the Body

The wind howled louder than when Cecil knocked on Aurora's front door earlier in the evening while Cecil carried two shovels and Aurora and Mr. Dexley held the tarp while they walked towards the woods. Cecil just couldn't believe the events unfolding before him. Unfortunately, Cecil didn't have time to argue with Aurora and her father. The decision was made, so Cecil needed to accept what they were about to do. It wasn't like Cecil wanted to desecrate Mom's memory. He, Aurora, and Mr. Dexley just didn't have any other options. No matter what way Cecil spun the situation, he realized he could get blamed for Mom's death. Being an orphan meant Cecil had to look out for himself—if he didn't nobody else would. And if that meant extra worrying and overanalyzing situations, then so be it.

An owl hooted while Cecil, Aurora, and Mr. Dexley approached the woods. Cecil almost dropped the shovels while his gaze remained on the owl resting on a nearby tree branch. Something menacing existed from the owl's glowing yellow eyes. Almost as if the owl wanted to wait for the perfect opportunity before attacking Cecil.

Cecil shook his head—he needed to get a grip. And fast. Owls didn't attack people, so Cecil would be fine. He was just a little extra sensitive in light of everything that happened in the last several hours.

"Are you coming, Cecil?" Aurora asked in the distance.

"Yeah, sorry." Cecil scurried past the owl and caught up with Aurora and her dad. Then, a bitter feeling lingered in his throat. At this rate, Aurora and Mr. Dexley must've thought Cecil was an idiot. And Cecil couldn't have that. They were doing him a favor, and Cecil refused to look like some bumbling fool. In theory, at least. A difference existed between believing in an idea and actually following through with said idea. Cecil of all people understood that idea. Mom made a lot of melodramatic comments over the course of Cecil's life, yet just because she said something didn't mean she'd actually do said thing.

Leaves crunched under Cecil's shoes while he once again found himself needing to catch up to Aurora and Mr. Dexley. He needed to work on the whole not getting distracted thing. No debate to be had about it.

Cecil took a deep breath several minutes later when he, Aurora, and Mr. Dexley arrived at the clearing in the woods. After that, Cecil dropped the shovels. Aurora and Mr. Dexley placed the tarp on the ground, then Mr. Dexley unraveled the tarp. Cecil cringed when Mom's headless body and head caught his attention. Burying Mom in the woods behind his house wasn't something that should happen. Not ever. However, this situation couldn't be changed. Mom died. And that was the current reality.

Mr. Dexley glanced at Cecil. "You can go back inside if you want. You shouldn't have to be here for this part."

"It's fine," Cecil murmured.

Aurora patted Cecil's shoulder. "You sure?"

Cecil shrugged. "It's not like I have anything better to do."

"That's a morbid way to look at things," Aurora said. "But hey. I'm guess I'm not one to talk since I'm helping to bury a body."

Cecil bit his lip. "Let's get this over with."

Mr. Dexley grabbed a shovel and started digging. Aurora snatched the other shovel and joined her father.

"We need to get the story straight," Cecil said.

Mr. Dexley drew in a breath. "There's not much to figure out. Your mother decided she wanted to travel, so she went on a long trip and left you with me."

"What about her job at the bakery?" Cecil asked. "Eventually, they're gonna wonder why my mom didn't show up to work."

Mr. Dexley's lips curled. "I'll speak to the owner tomorrow during my lunch break."

"Okay." Cecil tucked his hands behind his head.

"You're gonna need to get some of your stuff from your house," Mr. Dexley said. "I assume you have clothes and other possessions you want to bring with you when you move into my home?"

Cecil gave Mr. Dexley a cursory nod. Speaking wasn't something Cecil felt like doing at the moment. Concocting a plan and making sure nobody discovered Mom was dead shouldn't have happened. And goosebumps formed on Cecil's arms, back, and legs. Creepy was the only word that entered Cecil's mind when it came to the current situation.

"What about the school?" Aurora asked.

"I'll explain the situation about how Cecil is staying with us now," Mr. Dexley said.

Aurora's red hair bobbed in the wind. "Sounds good."

"What if Scarecrow returns?" Cecil finally asked.

"Then we'll deal with it when it happens," Mr. Dexley said.

Aurora coughed into her right arm. "What did you mean when you mentioned how Cecil's mother dying wasn't the first strange thing you heard about recently?"

"Doesn't matter," Mr. Dexley said.

Aurora giggled. "It seemed kinda important."

Mr. Dexley frowned. "I'd let you know if there was something you and Cecil needed to be aware of. Trust me."

Aurora huffed. "Whatever."

"We have a job to finish." Mr. Dexley placed Mom's head in the hole he and Aurora dug, then did the same with the rest of her body. It wasn't long before Mr. Dexley picked up one of the shovels and began throwing dirt over the hole.

Aurora looped her arms around Cecil, staring him down. "I know it doesn't seem like it right, but you'll get through this."

Mr. Dexley squealed. "Aurora's right."

"If you say so," Cecil said.

Aurora rubbed her hands together. "No offense, Dad, but your explanation doesn't cut it. I know you're up to something."

"Knowledge isn't always power," Mr. Dexley said.

Aurora snorted. "And what's that supposed to mean?"

"Exactly what I said it means," Mr. Dexley replied.

"You know something, don't you?" Aurora asked, raising her voice slightly.

"It's not important."

"It's not polite to keep secrets, Dad!"

"This isn't something you wanna know about!" Mr. Dexley remained silent for a moment. "Now please leave it alone!"

"I can't."

"Let's just say Cecil's imaginary friend might not be the only problem."

"And what's that supposed to mean?"

"Forget it."

"I want an explanation. It's the least Cecil and I deserve."

"Wow. Sometimes, I forget how similar you are to your mother with your persistence."

"Mom would want me to know the truth."

"I don't know about that."

Cecil stared into space while Aurora and Mr. Dexley droned on with their argument. If they didn't stop talking soon, then Cecil would get a headache. Their arguing wasn't accomplishing anything. And Cecil wasn't in the mood to listen to their banter.

***

"You don't have to be afraid to share your feelings with me," Aurora said while she and Cecil continued walking to school.

Cecil let out a nervous laugh. "I'm not afraid of anything."

"We both know that's not true."

"I know you're only trying to help, but I'm not exactly in the mood to chat about what happened last night. Someone can only do so much talking."

"Fair enough."

"And please don't say anything to the others—that wouldn't do any good. They'd just feel bad for me, which would be silly. Not like they can bring back Mom."

"Fair enough." Aurora gripped her backpack strap tighter. "But all joking aside, I at least hope you like your room."

"It's great."

"Okay. Good."

Grey clouds veiled the sky while Cecil and Aurora turned left and headed down a new road. The mysteries of life never ceased to amaze Cecil. The world was twisted, yet the current reality wasn't lost on Cecil. The gloomy sky matched his mood to a T. And Cecil hoped he and Aurora would get to school before it started raining. He didn't need to deal with both losing Mom and arriving at school in wet clothes. Doing so would've been unfair. So, Cecil prayed even the universe wouldn't be that nasty. Everyone deserved a break every now and then, including Cecil.

***

Cecil woke up, gasping. He had a nightmare reliving Mom's beheading. And his bad dream might have been his intuition trying to warn him. Scarecrow stood in front of him in Cecil's new bedroom at Aurora's place.

"What are you doing here?" Cecil demanded.

"I want to make a deal with you."

"I'm not interested in anything you've gotta say. You're a murderer, and that's all you'll ever be in my eyes."

"That's harsh!" Scarecrow quipped.

"It's not mean if it's true."

Scarecrow sighed. "Killing your mother was drastic. I'll admit that."

"It was downright evil."

"Why don't I just come here to say what I wanted to say?"

"Fine."

"If you accept me back into your life, then I won't harm anyone else you care about."

Cecil squinted. "Why should I believe you?"

"Because I always keep my word."

Cecil scowled. "That's laughable."

"You don't have to give me your answer now, but I'll be back soon."

"I look forward to it."

"Really?" Scarecrow asked, desperation radiating from his voice.

"No, I was being sarcastic."

Scarecrow narrowed his gaze. "I deserve better than snark."

"You don't deserve anything after you killed my mother."

"Let's agree to disagree."

Something clicked in Cecil's mind. Perhaps he had the power to destroy Scarecrow all along. Maybe, just maybe, the problem had a simple solution. Sometimes, difficult situations had easy resolutions, and a little perspective was the only thing required for dealing with a complex task such as a former imaginary friend hellbent on revenge.

Cecil cackled. "I can wish you away."

"Come again?"

"You heard me. I've got no use for you, and it's time for you to disappear forever."

Scarecrow remained in his current spot while rage bubbled inside Cecil—wishing Scarecrow away seemed like the logical solution. Scarecrow was an extension of Cecil, after all. So, if anyone could vanquish Scarecrow, then it should've been Cecil.

"What the heck?" Cecil stammered.

"I take it things didn't go as planned?"

"You shouldn't still be here."

"Whatever you say."

Cecil curled his fingers into a small fist. "Why didn't you disappear?"

"I'm your imaginary friend."

"What does that mean?"

Scarecrow squealed. "I'm tethered to you."

Cecil rubbed his jaw. He had a good idea of what Scarecrow hinted at, yet he didn't want to make false assumptions. Therefore, Scarecrow needed to be clearer. "Are you implying that me dying is the only way to kill you?"

"Maybe. Maybe not."

"That's not very helpful."

A scorching sensation returned to Cecil's stomach. To say Cecil felt foolish was an understatement. And that meant Cecil was right back where he started...grappling with the truce Scarecrow proposed.

"It's not my job to solve your problems...not anymore," Scarecrow said.

"That's mean!"

"It's the truth."

Cecil's shoulders twitched. "I can't believe I ever trusted you."

"Don't say that. In case you forgot, we had a lot of fun."

"Key word being, 'had,' as in the past."

"Whatever," Scarecrow mumbled.

"You'd really be okay with killing more innocent people if I don't accept your deal?" Cecil asked.

"It'd be for the greater good."

"Unbelievable!" Cecil exclaimed.

"Maybe one day you'll understand."

"Doubtful."

"Bye, Cecil." Scarecrow disappeared in a flash, not even making a crackling noise after vanishing.

Cecil grabbed the glass of water on the table by his bed, then finished it. Scarecrow's deal tempted Cecil more than the proposal should've—Cecil didn't want any more innocent blood shed. Yet Scarecrow's words seemed too good to be true. Scarecrow could double-cross Cecil and leave him looking foolish.

His jaw trembled. Boy, did Cecil hate how complicated life had gotten. His biggest problem should've been deciding what book to read before bed. Not navigating some sort of twisted revenge game with Scarecrow. It was some life, truly.

Another Death

The bell rang, and the majority of students flocked out of the classroom while Cecil shoved his notebook and textbook into his backpack. Nothing new, though. Cecil was always one of the last to leave class. And that was fine. He had bigger problems to contemplate. Like Mom dying. Or wheat would happen if he didn't let Scarecrow back into his life.

"Do you have a second to chat, Cecil?" Mr. Fickler asked from his desk.

Cecil looked upward while he zipped his backpack. An adult telling him that they needed to talk never seemed like a good thing. But Cecil wasn't in the mood to argue with Mr. Fickler or anyone else. Bickering wouldn't accomplish anything. Having words with someone seemed so trivial in light of everything that transpired in the last thirty-eight hours.

Mr. Fickler let out a small laugh. "Don't worry you...you didn't do anything wrong and aren't in trouble."

"Okay. No problem." Cecil walked over to Mr. Fickler, who still remained by his mahogany desk.

Mr. Fickler cleared his throat after Cecil's last classmate exited the room. "The main office told me about your situation."

"What now?"

"No need to be bashful. It's not a big deal."

"Huh?"

"I just wanted to let you know I'm here to chat if you ever feel like venting." Mr. Fickler played with his argyle tie.

"Thanks."

"It's okay for you to be angry about your mother wanting to travel and leaving you with Aurora and her father."

Disbelief washed over Cecil. He couldn't believe Mr. Dexley already notified the office about becoming his de facto guardian. Almost as if relaying that truth meant completing another step in the whole process of accepting Mom dying.

Cecil looked away from his teacher. "It is what it is."

"Do you mind if I speak freely?"

"Sure. Go ahead."

Cecil didn't mind humoring Mr. Fickler. At least Mr. Fickler attempted to be polite by inquiring if talking bluntly was okay. Doing so was more than most adults would've done. And for that, Cecil was thankful.

"I pride myself in being both a good judge of character and having a wonderful intuition," Mr. Fickler said.

"That's wonderful. But what does that have to do with me?"

"I don't want to put words in your mouth and make any false assumptions, but it also seems like you're holding back. I mean, you didn't even raise your hand once today. And you know I usually can't call on you because I realize you know the answer."

"Having an off day isn't a crime."

"No, it's not."

"I appreciate your concern, but everything is fine." Cecil pushed his backpack straps upward. Hopefully, the conversation would end soon.

Mr. Fickler chuckled. "When someone says they're fine, that usually means they aren't fine. But if you don't want to discuss whatever's bothering, then that's fine. I don't want you to share anything you aren't comfortable revealing. Just know my door is always open if you feel like chatting. I mean, I might not be able to make your life perfect. However, I can at least be a good listener. I'm sure I don't need to tell a smart boy like you about the dangers of bottling emotions up."

Regret pulsed through Cecil. In an ideal situation, he would've told Mr. Fickler about everything that happened. Yet Cecil couldn't bring himself to be honest with his teacher. Mr. Fickler knowing about what really happened wouldn't help.

Cecil's stomach grumbled. "Do you mind if I go to lunch now?'

"No problem."

"Although thanks for caring. That's rare these days, unfortunately."

"Don't mention it."

Cecil darted out of the classroom without glancing back at Mr. Fickler. Maybe, just maybe, Cecil would be okay. He hadn't spotted Scarecrow since he appeared in his bedroom afternoon the nightmare. And that meant his former imaginary best friend could've just been making an empty threat. Cecil hoped that was the case, at least. No hope was better than false hope. If Scarecrow really was after Cecil, then he didn't know what he'd do. Dealing with a deranged former imaginary friend wasn't something en eleven-year-old needed to deal with. In fact, the whole situation was beyond twisted.

***

Someone knocked on Cecil's bedroom door. He grabbed his bookmark, which lay right beside him on his pillow. Then, Cecil marked his spot in the book before grinning at Aurora, who held two mugs. No explanation necessary about how life would've been lonely without a best friend.

Aurora beamed. "I thought you might want some hot cocoa."

"Thanks." Cecil stood, then grabbed one of the mugs from Aurora. He almost sipped his chocolatey beverage, yet steam still rose from the cup. So, Cecil didn't feel like adding burning his tongue to his list of woes.

"I could ask how you're adjusting to living with Dad and me, but that might not be the smartest thing to ask right now."

"It's fine."

"You don't have to be brave for me, Cecil."

"I'll keep that in mind."

"I'm serious."

"No offense, but I'm kind of getting déjà vu at the moment."

"What do you mean?" Aurora asked.

"Mr. Fickler wanted to make sure I was okay in light of my mother traveling."

Her eyes widened. "You didn't tell him the truth, did you?"

"Of course, not. Don't be ridiculous."

"Phew."

"Do you think I'm an idiot, or something?"

"I never said that."

"But you implied it," Cecil said.

Aurora gave Cecil a weak smile. "Let's not fight."

"Okay. Okay."

"I'm sorry it happened the way it did, but I'm cool we're living together. Let's like a playdate or sleepover that never ends."

"True."

"And please don't worry about being a burden. My father and I are more than happy to have you live with us. Also, it's better than you living with some random stranger."

Cecil's spine should've tingled from Aurora's comment—having someone read his mind freaked him out. However, Cecil would make an exception for Aurora since she was one of his best friends. Genuine friendship entailed guessing what the other was thinking and Cecil wouldn't have it any other way. If Scarecrow really wanted revenge, then Cecil needed all the help he could fine.

"I wasn't telling you what you wanted to hear when we were in the woods," Aurora finally said.

"Come again?"

"Your life is gonna work out—I just know it."

"I'm glad you can be optimistic for both of us."

"There's no other way."

Cecil smirked. "Enough about me. Someone enjoyed playing amateur detective by grilling her father."

"I don't know what you're referring to."

"Don't play dumb with me. You're convinced your father is hiding something, so spill."

"There's nothing to tell. Dad made a comment about other strange things going besides your mother dying, and he's clearly holding back." Aurora sipped her hot cholate.

"You're gonna make it your mission to find out, though, right?"

"You know it."

Cecil's eyebrows shot up. "You don't think your father is hiding anything bad, do you?"

"I don't know, but I wish I did."

"Did you ever think this would be our life?"

"Not in a million years."

"Me neither."

"Adjusting our expectations doesn't mean life will turn out badly. It just might mean that things don't happen one percent according to plan." Aurora met Cecil's gaze. "I'm sorry. Was that mean of you? Because I wasn't trying to make light of your mother's death...I swear it."

"It's fine."

Cecil hadn't humored Aurora with his comment—he meant what he said. Accusing Aurora of being insensitive about Mom's death was like saying the sky was green. It just wasn't so.

"There were times I wanted an imaginary friend," Aurora said.

"Seriously?"

"For a fleeting moment, that was. Obviously, they can be more trouble than they're worth."

"You don't say."

A lump lingered in Cecil's throat—one he couldn't push down. "Your father can really afford to take on a second kid?"

"He makes more than you'd think running a pawn shop."

"Wow. Okay."

"I'm serious, Cecil."

"Relax, I believe you."

***

Cecil set in the back of Mr. Fickler's classroom while his teacher rambled. And with one tilt of his head, Cecil's heart raced. Scarecrow stood next to his desk, begging the question of what he wanted. Cecil had an idea of what Scarecrow might want. However, he wouldn't get himself worked up unless he absolutely had a reason to be nervous.

"You owe me an answer," Scarecrow said.

"I'm not letting you back into my life—not after you killed my mother," Cecil whispered. "And if you care about me, then you have a funny way of showing."

"That's your final answer?"

"Yup, we're done now."

"Okay then."

Cecil breathed a sigh of relief once Scarecrow vanished. Perhaps his hunch was right. Maybe, just maybe, Scarecrow made an empty threat about retaliating if he didn't let him back into his life.

The matter simmered in Cecil's mind for another beat. Yeah, life would be okay—it had to be. Mom dying proved more unpleasant than the time she forced him to try every vegetable in existence. But life could only improve from here.

Cecil's heart lurched when something grabbed his attention. More specifically, someone. Scarecrow stood behind Mr. Fickler, gripping an axe.

Scarecrow sniggered. "Don't say I didn't warn you."

Scarecrow swung his axe before Cecil could alert Mr. Fickler. And just like Mom, Mr. Fickler's head went flying before making a loud thump when landing on the ground.

Blood oozed from Mr. Fickler's headless body while everyone in the class screamed. Unfortunately for Cecil, Scarecrow killed again. And there was no telling who Scarecrow's next target might be.

A Midnight Stroll

"It's important we have this discussion now before your father comes from work," Cecil said while he and Aurora stood in the kitchen.

"Let me guess. You wanna chat about what happened Mr. Fickler?"

"Yup."

Aurora bit her lip. "I'm glad I was in the bathroom when the incident happened. I can't imagine witnessing a beheading."

"Scarecrow killed Mr. Fickler," Cecil blurted.

Her gaze narrowed. "What did you just say?"

"You heard me." Cecil nibbled on the inside of his lip. "No offense or anything, but didn't you connect the dots with how Mr. Fickler is the second beheading in the less than a week?"

Aurora nodded. "Good point."

Cecil wailed. "It's all my fault. Maybe Scarecrow would've spared Mr. Fickler if I let him back in my life. I mean, Mr. Fickler's innocent. He didn't deserve to be caught up in my drama with scarecrow."

Another pang of guilt overwhelmed Cecil. Not trusting Scarecrow proved smart in theory. However, Cecil had emotions like anyone else. And that meant Cecil wondered what would've happened if he accepted Scarecrow's truce. Mom dying terrified Cecil enough as it was. But now, Cecil had another death on his conscience.

Aurora heaved a sigh. "You can't blame yourself, Cecil. You aren't responsible for the actions of your former BFF."

"Thanks for saying that."

"It's the truth. Blaming yourself also won't accomplish anything. What we need is a plan. Perhaps my father can help us."

Cecil's eye bulged. "We can't tell your dad that Scarecrow killed a second person."

"Why not?" Aurora demanded. "At this point, we've got nothing to lose."

"What's your father gonna do?"

"He could tell us what he's been keeping from us."

Cecil let out a forced laugh. "You're never gonna let that go?"

"My dad is hiding something. I'd bet my life on it."

"Be careful. I wouldn't want Scarecrow to hear you."

"I'm not afraid of Scarecrow."

"Hubris isn't a good look. I'd hate for you to eat those words."

Aurora glared. "Anyone ever tell you spend way too much time reading books?"

Cecil winked. "Jealous you don't know what hubris means?"

"Please. As if."

"I'll take that as a yes."

"You can take that however you want. However, that doesn't change how you have a deranged imaginary friend after you."

"Don't remind me!" Cecil exclaimed.

"Well, that's where we're at. And the sooner we get rid of Scarecrow, the sooner our lives can go back to normal."

"If only life were that simple."

Aurora's face drooped. "I can understand if you're reluctant to involve my father in your situation with Scarecrow. But there's something else you should consider. Roman, Lena, and Jace have a right to know about Scarecrow."

"Why?"

"They could become his next target. I mean, a little warning would be nice. Could you live with yourself if something happened to them?"

Cecil appreciated the general point of Aurora's comment, yet he could've done without the guilt-trip. That wasn't something Cecil deserved. Not in light of how complicated his life had become recently. At the end of the day, Cecil had to live his life, not Aurora. And he wouldn't be bullied into doing something just because Aurora said he should.

The request remained on Cecil's mind while a silence ensued between them. Aurora's insistent attitude might annoy even the most good-natured person. But at the end of the day, her point about how Roman, Jace, and Lena might become collateral damage wasn't lost on him. Cecil would feel awful if something happened to his friends and he hadn't given them a proper about Scarecrow. If Scarecrow wanted to target his pals, then they deserved a fighting chance. It was what Cecil would've wanted if the situation were reversed. And one of his friends had an enemy that might target him.

Aurora coughed into her arm. "I didn't say what I did to upset you. It's just that there's strength in numbers."

"Understood."

"And if it makes you feel better, I don't think they're gonna judge you for having an imaginary friend."

"Okay. Okay."

A small smile tugged at the corner of Aurora's lips. "And I'm not giving up on my father. He's bound to slip up eventually about whatever secret he's keeping."

"If you say so."

"I know so."

Cecil scratched the side of his head. "There's one thing that bothers me about the situation more than anything."

"And what's that?"

"How do you deal with enemy like Scarecrow?"

"I'm not following you..."

"There's no telling when Scarecrow might pop up, which means he has the element of surprise."

"Well, that's a fair point. But the truth is a good place start. And not because I think lying by omission or telling an occasional fib is bad, I don't. We just need more people on our side, and we'll get that once Roman, Jace, and Lena know the truth."

"Will you help me tell them?"

Aurora didn't so much as blink. "Yes, I will."

"Thanks, I appreciate that."

"That's why I'm your best friend, silly. If you can't count on me to help you with your situation with Scarecrow, then who can you count on?"

Cecil snickered. "Good point."

"What about right now? Scarecrow isn't here with us?"

"What are you getting at?"

"I'm just trying to understand how this whole thing works," Aurora said.

"No, Scarecrow isn't here with us right now."

"Well, that's a relief." Aurora elevated her eyebrows. "So, you were the only one who saw Scarecrow when he killed Mr. Fickler?"

"Correct."

"Okay then."

"Yeah, the whole thing is beyond weird."

Aurora clapped her hands. "Why don't we make hot cocoa?"

Wind slammed into the house so loudly that Cecil could've sworn he thought someone screamed. And that proved when Aurora was right, she was right. Winter wasn't the only time of year to drink hot cocoa. There were plenty of cold days during other times of the year. Because that was the thing about weather. It changed on a moment's notice like almost everything else in life. In the morning it could be warm and sunny. Then, it could be rainy and windy in the afternoon. And that uncertainty was what frightened Cecil most. Nothing fun with not knowing what would happen next, almost as if that doubt created a sense of helplessness.

***

Cecil went for a stroll while stars illuminated the night sky. Aurora and Mr. Dexley had already gone to bed, so Cecil thought it'd be harmless if he went for a midnight stroll in the woods. Scarecrow would probably do what he wanted regardless, proving it didn't matter what time of day it was. In light of the Scarecrow situation, no safe time of day existed. Bad things happened in both daylight and during the night. Mom and Mr. Fickler's deaths proved that. Mom died in the evening whereas Mr. Fickler perished during the morning.

Someone cackled. "A little morbid to go walking around past your bedtime, don't you think?"

Cecil craned his neck. Great. Another Scarecrow encounter was the last thing he wanted or needed. And Cecil hoped there'd be no more bloodshed. Two innocent people dying proved grizzly enough, so Cecil wouldn't have words to describe if Scarecrow killed a third innocent person.

"You could at least acknowledge me," Scarecrow said.

"I generally make it a habit not to associate with murderers."

"Ouch."

"What I said is true."

"I was serious, Cecil." Scarecrow squealed louder. "A nice boy such as yourself shouldn't be out this late."

"Why? Are you gonna kill me?"

Scarecrow remained silent.

"That's what I thought," Cecil continued. "Anyway, it'd be nice if you answered one of my questions."

"Ask me anything you want. I have nothing to hide."

"Why wait till now to get revenge?"

"I was hoping you'd see the error of your ways."

Cecil gave Scarecrow an icy look. "You still haven't told me what your endgame is."

"That's for me to know and you to find out."

"Are you gonna kill my friends?'

"Maybe. Maybe not."

Cecil fretted. "Mr. Fickler was innocent. He didn't deserve to die."

"I needed to send a message."

"What happened to you?" Cecil asked. "You aren't the same being I met shortly after my father died."

"You happened to me."

"And what's that supposed to mean?"

Scarecrow made a hissing noise. "You used me then casted me aside like I was nothing."

"I didn't have a choice. My mother was threatening to send me a way if I didn't cut you out of my life."

"You don't abandon your real friends."

Cecil rolled his eyes. "You can believe what you want. However, I never took you for granted."

"Doubtful."

"Have you forgotten how you wouldn't have existed without me?"

"Don't say that!" Scarecrow roared.

"Not my fault if you can't handle the truth."

Scarecrow grumbled. "I'm real even if I don't exist in the traditional sense. And in time, you'll understand that."

Cecil folded his arms. "Where were you for the year you were gone?"

"Doesn't matter. Because I'm out of here."

"Guess you don't care about me if you're leaving."

"That's not true, and you know it. I just have things to do, and people to see."

Cecil made a pig-like snort. "If you say so."

Scarecrow leaned forward, and an icy sensation washed over Cecil. "Hope ditching me was worth it, because you haven't even begun to suffer yet. I'm just getting warmed up. And by the time I'm done with you, you won't recognize Hicklewapper."

"Wow. I'm so scared."

"You should be." Scarecrow snapped his fingers, then vanished as quickly as he appeared to Cecil in the woods.

Something howled in the distance, and Cecil yelped. He hated to think a deer, elk, or rabbit got attacked by some larger predator like a coyote. Interacting with Scarecrow moments earlier meant Cecil hit his morbid quota for the night.

Cecil shook his head, then headed back in the direction he came from while a twig snapped. Perhaps Cecil needed a good night sleep. Scarecrow couldn't harm Cecil while he slept. He hoped not, at least. Cecil's bedroom at Aurora's house was the only sanctuary he had left. And he refused to let Scarecrow take that from him.

Truth Time

Cecil's pulse drummed in his ears while Aurora remained by his side and Roman, Lena, and Jace stood in front of him in an empty school hallway before homeroom. Somehow, Cecil would tell Roman, Lena, and Jace the truth about Scarecrow even if admitting the truth spooked him more than having to repeat a grade. Roman, Lena, and Jace deserved to know the truth. Cecil refused to be a coward. Not because he cared about being judged by others, but because Cecil cared about setting himself to a certain standard— Cecil needed to be happy with what he saw when he looked in the mirror.

"What's going on?" Lena pushed her frayed headband further up her forehead. "No offense or anything, but I need to catch up on my homework before homeroom."

Roman smirked. "Whatever happened to doing homework at home?"

Jace elbowed Roman. "Knock it off!"

"Fine," Roman said. "If you wanna defend your girlfriend, then that's your business. But don't be rude. Cecil wouldn't ask us to meet if weren't important."

"Lena isn't my girlfriend," Jace snapped, face turning bright red. "I'm way too young to think about dating."

Roman chuckled. "Whatever."

Lena shifted her weight towards Cecil. "Are you gonna answer Roman's question, or what? What you you've gotta say is important, right?'

"Yes," Cecil forced out.

"Well?" Lena pressed, voice echoing through the hallway.

"I'm being stalked by my former imaginary BFF," Cecil said. "My mother isn't away traveling—Scarecrow beheaded her. And he also killed Mr. Fickler."

"You for real?" Jace asked.

A cold expression remained plastered on Aurora's face. "It's the truth. And it's a good thing Cecil told you."

"Wait," Lena stammered. "You knew before us?"

"Duh," Aurora said. "Why do you think Cecil is staying with my father and me?"

Jace furrowed his brow. "Why tell us about Scarecrow?"

"Have you not been listening?" Cecil asked. "You guys could be next. And I couldn't live with myself if something happened to you."

"I see," Lena mumbled.

Aurora sneered. "Not everything requires some snarky comment."

Cecil's breathing slowed down, returning to normal. Good to know Aurora would always defend him. No explanation necessary about how the world always proved to be a cruel place. Just no telling what bad thing might next.

"Well, you don't have to deal with this situation alone," Roman said.

Cecil beamed. "I don't?"

Roman let out a small. "No, silly. We'll help you deal with Scarecrow. That's what friends are for, right?"

"Right," Aurora said.

Jace nodded. "Agreed."

Aurora's gaze shifted towards Lena.

"Oh, fine," Lena finally said.

"It won't be easy," Cecil said.

Roman gaped. "I wouldn't expect anything less."

"I'd like to know how we're supposed to go about defeating an imaginary friend," Lena said. "That's not something that happens every day."

"I was thinking of checking out the library—maybe there's a book that can help us." Aurora flipped her hair over her shoulders. "Plus, I might pick my dad's brain. He might be able to help us."

Cecil almost grinned. Wanting to go to the library illustrated a logical response. And Cecil appreciated Aurora's calmness. If they wanted to defeat Scarecrow, then one of the them needed to be levelheaded.

Lena gave Aurora a weird look. "Do you know something we don't?"

"Maybe," Aurora murmured.

Lena winked. "Then you should share."

"I'll let you guys know when I discover something important," Aurora said.

Roman chuckled. "Fair enough."

"I'm not kidding," Aurora said.

"Relax," Roman said. "I believe you."

"I should hope so," Aurora said.

"Do you ever not worry?" Roman asked.

Aurora laced her fingers together. "Sometimes."

"Well, I'm sure we'll be able to defeat Scarecrow," Roman said.

Lena rolled her eyes. "We better."

Aurora resumed her rambling while relief bubbled inside Cecil. Life was less than ideal, yet having his friends support him pleased Cecil more than a day off from school. Cecil would find a way to defeat Scarecrow, he just knew it. Determination and tenacity counted for more than people realized. And Cecil wouldn't accept defeat. Mom and Mr. Fickler deserved that much. The only question was how they'd defeat Scarecrow. Lena annoyed Cecil more than he cared to admit. However, she was right. Defeating a former imaginary friend wasn't an ordinary task. So, whether they got answers from Aurora's library research or her pestering her father, Cecil hoped they'd find a solution. Returning to simpler times was what Cecil craved most. And that wouldn't happen until they defeated Scarecrow.

Up in Flames

Cecil sat in the back of the classroom while Mr. Fickler's replacement (Mr. Hickler) rambled on with the history lesson. And if Scarecrow didn't presently occupy most of his current thoughts, then Cecil might laugh about how Mr. Fickler and Mr. Hickler had the same last name save for one letter difference. Yet Cecil didn't have it in to think about much other than Scarecrow. He still couldn't believe what his current life entailed. His reasoning wasn't about feeling sorry for himself. Cecil just couldn't comprehend why some of his classmates always beamed and smiled while he struggled getting through every waking second.

Counting to ten in his head was the only thing Cecil could do. Telling his friends about Scarecrow proved smart. Not only because Lena, Jace, and Roman deserved to know a homicidal imaginary friend might mess with him. But also, because there was strength in numbers. His heart sank. Mom always bombarded him with that saying. And Cecil couldn't help feeling guilty for all the times he teased her about sounding corny or cliché.

Mr. Hickler shifted his weight. "Would you mind going to the supply closet down the hallway, Cecil? We're out of tissues."

"Sure thing." Cecil stood, then shuffled out of the classroom. He even did his best to ignore his clenched jaw. Getting a mini break from class might do him some good. However, Cecil hoped his preoccupied mind hadn't been that obvious to Mr. Hickler. It was nothing personal, truly. Cecil just didn't have it in him to care about school. Maybe one day, sure. But not anytime soon. His education seemed so futile in light of both his parents being dead. A chill soon rolled up his back. Being an orphan wasn't something Cecil would accept anytime soon. And he didn't know how he'd live with never being able to see his parents again. Forever was a long time. Especially when Cecil was only thirteen.

Cecil rounded the corner in the hallway and approached the supply closet. He opened the door, sighing in relief. The room wasn't locked, and Cecil was glad about that. Then, he'd have to make an extra trip. And Cecil didn't want that even if most of his classmates would've given almost anything to miss as much class time as possible. Flicking on the closet light hadn't done anything to stop the trepidation pulsing through him. Something claustrophobic existed from being inside such a small space. So, Cecil had a mission. Get the tissues. And get out.

The only problem was Cecil couldn't find the tissues. Perhaps the school forgot to restock the tissues. That explanation was the only logical conclusion Cecil could think of as to why there weren't any tissues in the supply closet.

"Looking for these," someone said.

Cecil spun around. Scarecrow stood in front of him several feet away, holding the tissues. And Cecil almost screamed. He couldn't leave the supply closet without passing by Scarecrow, so his former imaginary BFF trapped him.

"What are you doing here?" Cecil demanded.

"Is that any way to greet an old friend?"

Cecil crossed his arms. "You aren't my friend."

"We'll see about that."

"What are you doing here?"

"I wanted to check up on you. Is that a crime?"

"It is if you intend to do something illegal."

"Relax, I'm not gonna hurt you." Scarecrow paused for a beat. "I'm just in the mood to play a couple of games."

Scarecrow snapped his fingers with his free hand. A sea of red, orange, and yellow engulfed the tissue box. When the fire dissipated not even ashes were left behind.

Cecil raised his eyebrows. "Did you really have to do that?"

"It's more fun this way."

"You said you like games, right?"

Scarecrow nodded. "Correct."

"Then how can I play if I don't know what the rules are?"

"What are you babbling about?"

"I still have no idea where you were during the absence."

Scarecrow screeched. "I was in the desert with all the other discarded imaginary friends."

"There are others?"

"Duh."

"Wow, guess it's true what they say. You really do learn something new every day."

"There's a lot of selfish brats out there, unfortunately. But hey. At least you're in good company."

"I'm not selfish. I just had to move on with my life. Surely, you can understand that? I mean, it wouldn't kill you to be a little more grateful. I'm the person who gave you life, after all."

"Guilt tripping me isn't nice."

"So, what? Now that you burned the tissues, you're gonna kill me?"

"Not exactly."

"Then what?" Cecil asked, voice bouncing against the walls.

"Let's just say it's time to turn up the heat." Scarecrow snapped his fingers, and a canister levitated in mid-air. Then, the container emptied its contents. It wasn't long until a matchbook appeared.

"Scarecrow, no!"

"It's too late for groveling."

The match lit itself, and it dropped onto the ground. Flames spread across the room and sweat dripped down Cecil's face. And Cecil didn't care if his perspiration was because of his increased nerves or because of the fire's warm temperature was starting to get to him. Finding a way out of the supply closet was his only option.

Scarecrow squealed. "I could help you, but that'd require letting me back into your life full time. And something tells me that's not something you're ready to do."

"Well, looks like you aren't wrong about everything."

"I didn't want it to be this way."

"Serious?" Cecil asked.

"Don't despair. I'm sure your death will be quick."

Cecil's pulse drummed in his ears. Scarecrow annoyed him, yet he wasn't totally wrong. Dying was what would happen if he didn't find a way out of the supply closet. So, Cecil had to figure a way out of his predicament like yesterday.

Cecil tilted his head. He couldn't exit the room the way he entered—the fire encompassed the majority of the supply closet. Yet there was a window by him. And Cecil could go out the window. Being on the second floor meant there wasn't that much of a drop to the ground. Besides, it was only a garden beneath the window. So, maybe, just maybe, the garden might cushion his fall. It was a nice idea, anyway. Actually, this plan was the only one Cecil had. And that meant Cecil had to give it a shot. He owed himself that much.

The fire crackled louder, snapping Cecil out of his contemplation. He ran to the window, attempting to open it. Except the window wouldn't budge.

"Something wrong?" Scarecrow asked.

"No, everything's fine. I just need to give it a little more elbow grease."

Lying was Cecil's best option. The current moment wasn't the time for showing weakness. Panic was a weapon Scarecrow could exploit. And Cecil wouldn't allow that. Not now. Not ever. Not if he wanted to live.

Cecil mumbled a profanity under his breath. The window refused to open, and Cecil didn't know what he'd do. His obituary couldn't read that he died in a fire started by his imaginary friend. Being only thirteen years old meant Cecil had a lot of life left in him. And Cecil refused to be outsmarted by his former imaginary friend.

His face lit up. There was a shovel on the adjacent shelf, so Cecil grabbed the tool and smacked it against the window as hard as he could. Nothing happened, so Cecil thwacked the glass one more time with the shovel. Glass shattered onto the ground. Cecil leapt out the window, praying everything would be okay.

He thudded against the ground a moment later. Yet his body didn't ache. He opened his eyes. Cecil lay in the garden like he anticipated.

Glee trickled through Cecil's body. For once, something went right. And he couldn't help the enthusiasm bubbling inside him. There was a brief moment when Cecil thought he wouldn't make it, yet he got a reprieve. And this miracle was worth everything in the world.

Remaining at school didn't appeal to Cecil, though. He needed a break, so he ran. And he ran. And he ran. Going home was the only thing that currently appealed to Cecil. Nearly burning to death killed any fleeting joy he might've gotten from school.

***

"I'm sorry about what happened to you," Aurora said hours later while she and Cecil sat on wooden stools by the kitchen counter, enjoying their hot cocoa.

"Don't worry about it."

"No need to put on a façade for me. What you went through sucked."

"Thanks."

Aurora nudged Cecil. "I'm being serious."

"Hopefully, your dad can smooth things over with the school. I can't imagine they're happy about me ditching."

"It's not a big deal. I would've done the same thing."

Cecil made eye contact with Aurora. "There's something I wanted to ask you, although it might be awkward."

"And what's that?"

"Have you made any progress with finding out what your dad might be keeping from us? Because we could certainly use some good news."

Aurora bit her lip. "I'm afraid not."

"I see."

Aurora remained silent. Not that Cecil blamed her or anything—he didn't. Some situations were beyond words. And his current conversation with Aurora was one of those moments. Scarecrow trying to kill Cecil earlier in the day shouldn't have been part of Cecil's new normal, yet it was. And Cecil wished he had time to throw a tantrum about that.

"I don't mean to be rude or anything, but I think we're just gonna have to be direct with your father," Cecil continued. "If he knows something that could help us, then he needs to spill. We can't keep going on like this,"

"I know. I know."

An Almost Drowning

Cecil and his friends sat on their towels while the distinct aroma of salt water wafted through the air. Having a day off from school—it was a teacher development day—meant only one thing. Spending the day at the beach. And Cecil wouldn't have it any other way. In fact, Cecil couldn't remember the last time he went to the beach. Probably before Mom died. So, it was only natural that some sadness might linger inside him from the realization that Mom would never be able to enjoy something simple again like going to the beach. However, Cecil refused to kill the mood. There was a time and place for most things, including how Mom's beheading remained etched in his mind. Yet hanging with his friends on their day off wasn't the time or place to bring up how his grief often caused contradictory emotions. No, dissecting that issue could wait till later. There wasn't a cloud in the sky, which meant the weather complimented their day and off. Therefore, Cecil would've been crazy not to try and enjoy the outing. If all else failed the expression about making it till he faked it applied.

Perhaps Cecil believed he was having a good time, then he might actually have fun with his friends. Nice idea, anyway.

Roman looked towards Cecil's direction. "Everything okay, buddy? You've been more quiet than usual."

"You don't have to make a big deal out of everything," Aurora touted.

"Roman's only asking because he cares," Lena said.

Jace glared at Lena. "Since when do you speak for Roman?"

"Lighten up. I was only making an observation." Lena's hair bobbed in the wind.

"Whatever," Jace mumbled.

A small smile tugged at Roman's lips. "Wanna go in the water, Cecil?"

Cecil sighed. "Maybe later. But don't let me stop you."

"Fair enough.' Roman got up, then headed towards the water.

In a perfect world, Cecil would've joined Roman in the water. Yet life would never be ideal. It couldn't. Cecil was no closer to defeating Scarecrow. And to say Cecil was unhappy about that would've been an understatement. He and his friends needed a plan to defeat Scarecrow once and for all. There had to be a way to rid Hicklewapper of Scarecrow, Cecil just didn't know what it was. Yeah, his situation would work out. It had to. Riding the world of a menace like Scarecrow was the best way to honor Mom.

Aurora leaned towards Cecil's right ear. "Why didn't you wanna go in the water with Roman? You've never passed on an opportunity to spend quality with Roman."

Cecil pursed his lips. "And what's that supposed to mean?"

"Nothing, really. Just couldn't help noticing the way you two interact with each other. And I wanted to let you know it's not a big deal."

"It's not polite to whisper!" Lena quipped.

Jace beamed. "Lena's right."

"Mind your business!" Aurora said, raising her voice slightly.

"Okay then," Lena said.

"We need to come up with a plan about Scarecrow," Cecil said through gritted teeth. "And fast. We can't let anyone else get hurt."

Aurora huffed. "I know. I know."

"I'm serious, Aurora!" Cecil exclaimed.

Lena pushed a lock of her hair to the side. "If you two are mumbling about how you're gonna defeat Scarecrow, then please clue Jace and me in. A little warning would be the polite thing to do."

Aurora rolled her eyes. "The world doesn't revolve around you, Lena!"

Lena giggled. "It'd be nice if it did."

Cecil let out a small laugh. Sometimes, his emotions were beyond his control. His body should've remained tensed until he and his friends defeated Scarecrow. Yet even Cecil craved escapism. Even if it was something mundane such as Lena and Aurora's banter. Almost as if their petty arguing reminded Cecil of simpler times. At this rate, life before Scarecrow seemed like several lifetimes ago.

Aurora patted Cecil's back. "Do me a favor. Try and enjoy yourself—it's not every day we have the beach to ourselves."

"Duly noted," Cecil said.

Cecil glanced towards the water while he stretched his arms. Roman grinned at him. However, Cecil's heart soon lurched. Scarecrow appeared behind Roman.

Cecil screamed. "Roman, look out!"

Scarecrow dunked Roman's head into the water. Cecil looked on, horrified. If he and his friends don't do something, then Roman would drown. And Cecil refused to accept that possibility. Mom and

Mr. Fickler dying proved bad enough. A third death would've been unspeakable.

Lena snorted. "Why is Roman waving his arms in the air like he's pretending to drown?"

"Because Scarecrow is trying to kill him, you idiot!" Cecil stood, then rushed towards the water. He'd apologize to Lena later about losing his patience with forgetting how he was the only one who could see and hear Scarecrow. Saving Roman was the only thing that currently mattered. There was no guarantee Cecil would be successful, yet he had to try. Perhaps Scarecrow being tethered to him meant Cecil was the person who had the greatest chance to defeat him.

He entered the water, not even caring about the cold water jolting his body from the shock of the temperature not being warmer. He needed to free Roman. And fast. Every second counted when dealing with life and death situations.

Cecil sucked in a deep breath, and punched Scarecrow. Attacking his former imaginary friend was about saving Roman—not thinking violence was the solution to every problem. So, Cecil hoped he wouldn't be judged too harshly for doing what needed to be done to save Roman. In this case, hand to hand combat was the only way to deal with Scarecrow.

A splashing noise rippled through the water when Cecil knocked Scarecrow off Roman. Cecil pulled Roman's head out of the water, then dragged Roman to shore.

"What just happened?" Roman asked once he and Cecil were out of the water.

"Scarecrow tried to kill you."

"Wow…"

"I'm sorry, Roman."

"It's not your fault."

"Scarecrow's only targeting you to get my attention."

Roman snickered. "Well, it worked."

"Don't make jokes. You almost died."

"It's good to laugh about these things."

Cecil gave Roman a skeptical look. "I'm not so sure about that."

"The important thing is I'm okay."

"Yeah, that's true." Cecil took in a deep breath. "But we should find something else to do today. The beach doesn't seem like the best place to be when a homicidal lunatic is after me."

"If you insist." Roman blushed. "But seriously. Thanks again for saving my life. That's the kindest thing anyone has ever done for me."

"It's not a big deal."

"Don't be modest, Cecil. You did a really brave thing, and I'm not gonna forget what you did anytime soon."

***

Cecil curled his fingers into a small fist and knocked on Aurora's bedroom door. In light of Roman almost dying, he didn't have a choice with what he was about to ask Aurora. Maybe if the circumstances were different, then they wouldn't have to involve Aurora's father. Yet they weren't. Cecil could only deal with the situation at hand. So, Cecil and Aurora had to uncover what weird thing Mr. Dexley hinted at the night Cecil's mother died. And if what Mr. Dexley was keeping from them turned out to be a red herring and nothing to do with Scarecrow, at least Cecil would know he tried. The only thing worse than complaining was doing nothing, after all. Because Cecil would've rather Scarecrow forced him to eat his eyes than just continue twiddling his thumbs in hopes Mr. Dexley might feel generous and decide what was behind that cryptic comment the night Mom died. No, passiveness was never the right move. Cecil was in a position to do something about his predicament, so he would.

"Come in," Aurora finally said.

Cecil entered Aurora's bedroom, finding her by her desk. Aurora closed her book, then shifted her focus.

"What's up?" Aurora asked.

"We've gotta speak to your father about what he might be hiding. Today it was Roman who almost died. Tomorrow it could be you, Lena, or Jace."

"Yeah, you're probably right. It's not like I discovered anything useful in the library. I mean, the school has a lot of books. But dealing with imaginary friends or creatures technically aren't real wasn't one of the books."

"Hopefully, your father won't be too angry with us."

"He shouldn't."

***

Cecil, Aurora, and Mr. Dexley sat at the dining room table, enjoying apple pie. And like past situations, Cecil had to put aside his feelings. The irony wasn't lost on Cecil about how he and Mom were going to have apple pie before Scarecrow killed her. And a part of Cecil would always hate how he never got to have the last apple pie Mom baked. However, he and Aurora had a mission. Uncover what Mr. Dexley was hiding in hopes that whatever he was keeping from him and Aurora might be connected to Scarecrow.

"We can't dance around the truth any longer, Dad." Aurora broke off a small bite of her slice of apple pie and scarfed it down in a matter of seconds. "Things with Scarecrow have escalated. So, if you know something that could help Cecil, then you need to tell him."

Mr. Dexley's eyes widened. "You aren't gonna leave it alone, are you?"

Aurora smirked. "Nope. The night Cecil's mother died you mentioned that not being the only recent weird thing. And I'd like to know what you meant."

Mr. Dexley banged his fist against the table. "I don't know why you can't leave it alone, Aurora. What I was referring to had nothing to do with Cecil."

Cecil flinched. Mr. Dexley was flawed like everyone else. Yet Cecil didn't enjoy seeing this different side to Aurora's father. Being the grownup meant Mr. Dexley needed to be the calm one.

"I doubt that," Aurora said.

Mr. Dexley rolled his eyes. "Fine. You wanna know what I was referring to? Several of my friends thought their loved ones were sending them signs from the afterlife."

Aurora blinked. "That's it?"

"What do you mean that's it?" Mr. Dexley demanded. "You think you of all people would be sensitive to that matter."

Cecil's gaze remained on his dessert. It didn't matter if he wasn't the one in the hotseat. He'd never get used to that uneasy feeling swirling in his stomach when Aurora argued with her father. Cecil didn't quite know what of make of Aurora and Mr. Dexley being comfortable enough to argue in front of him. On the one hand, the openness flattered Cecil. Possibly having to leave the room every time Aurora and her minced words was no way to live. On the other hand, a little discretion wouldn't have killed Aurora and Mr. Dexley. Cecil would've been mortified if a stranger witnessed he and Mom bicker.

Not everything was meant for public consumption. Sometimes, a little mystery was a good thing.

"Mom has nothing to do with this," Aurora said.

Mr. Dexley resumed eating his apple pie.

"Why the secrecy, though?" Aurora asked.

"I didn't feel comfortable betraying their confidence," Mr. Dexley said. "Grief is a highly personal matter."

"Did you believe them?" Aurora slouched.

Mr. Dexley gave his daughter a disapproving look. "It doesn't matter what I believe. The point is, these signs brought comfort to my friends."

Cecil nibbled on the inside of his lip. "Are you telling me we're no closer to finding a way to defeat Scarecrow?"

"I'm afraid not," Mr. Dexley said.

Aurora shook her head. "Well, this was a complete let down."

Aurora's comment lingered in Cecil's mind—he couldn't argue with her. Mr. Dexley's secrecy the night Mom died turned out to be a big nothing burger. And Cecil hated that. He needed answers about defeating Scarecrow, yet didn't have the faintest clue about where to go finding them. His life was so perfect. Not.

REPRIEVE

Cecil stood by his locker before homeroom, getting the things he needed for his morning classes. His throat tightened while he shoved his notebooks and textbooks into his backpack. Just like Mom's death would always be etched in his mind, the same would also be said for Roman's near-death experience. Scarecrow trying to drown Roman wasn't something Cecil expected, yet Scarecrow had. So, Cecil needed to be more prepared for Scarecrow in the future. The only problem was Cecil still had no idea about how to defeat Scarecrow. And that sucked. Teachers always gave a disapproving look when a student said, "I don't know" when called on. Therefore, Cecil understood why teachers might get frustrated with certain students. Doubt and uncertainty never inspired much confidence, after all.

The slamming of his locker echoed through the hallway, and Cecil sighed in relief. There were a few other students standing in the hallway, yet nobody gave Cecil a dirty look about how he closed the locker too loudly. Attracting attention was the last thing Cecil wanted or needed. And that meant having to be more careful in the future.

He shook his head. The disbelief flooding his body never got old, and Cecil didn't know what he'd do about that feeling. Like it or not, this feud with former imaginary friend defined Cecil's life now.

"Hi stranger," someone said.

Cecil gave Aurora a small smile. "Hi."

Aurora's eyebrows inched up. "You didn't feel like waiting for me to walk to school?"

"I had a lot on my mind."

"Don't worry about it. I'm only teasing."

"Good."

Aurora tucked a lock of hair behind her ear. "I'm glad the others aren't here, though. There's something I wanted to chat with you about."

"And what's that?"

"I didn't mean to make you feel uncomfortable that day at the beach."

Cecil might've had a vague idea about what Aurora hinted at with her comment. However, she needed to be more specific. Cecil had enough to deal with because of the Scarecrow situation. And that meant he didn't have time to play guessing games. If Aurora wanted to make a point, then she needed to make it. Only fair. No explanation necessary about how wasting people's time got tiresome quickly.

Cecil's cheeks flushed. "I don't know what you're getting at, so you're gonna have to be more specific—no offense or anything."

"I've seen the way you and Roman stare at each other," Aurora said. "Almost kinda like the way Lena and Jace look at each other."

"It's not a crime to exchange stolen glances."

"Didn't say it was."

"I'm still not getting your point."

"You don't have to be embarrassed about it, Cecil."

Cecil's eyes widened. "Have you been eating your father's vitamins again?"

"This isn't a joke, Cecil!" Aurora quipped. "It's okay if you have a crush on Roman. I don't think he'd mind."

Cecil gave Aurora an icy look. "Not so loud!"

"Sorry."

"It's crazy you think I have a crush on Roman. You couldn't be further from the truth, and I wish you'd stop getting these weird ideas."

"If you can deal with coming out at eleven, then you can deal with this." Aurora tugged at her backpack strap. "I'm sure Roman would be flattered if he knew you like him as more than a friend. Who knows. Maybe he even feels the same way."

Cecil nibbled on the inside of his lip. "Telling my truth about how I'm bisexual isn't the same as admitting I have a crush on a friend."

"No, it's not." Aurora paused for a beat. "Are you afraid of losing Roman as a friend? Because like I said, there's a good chance for the situation to break in your favor."

"I can't be thinking about a silly crush!" Cecil barked. "Not when my life is at stake. Heck, the future of Hicklewapper might be on the line too."

"You fear rejection, don't you?"

"Don't psychoanalyze me. Your mother being a psychiatrist doesn't give you the right to therapy speak."

Aurora looked away the second Cecil's words left his mouth. It wasn't long before regret panged through Cecil. Perhaps mentioning Aurora's dead mother was mean. Certain subjects would always be off limits, after all. So, maybe, just maybe, Cecil needed to be more sensitive in the future. Something to consider, at least.

"I'm sorry," Cecil continued. "I shouldn't have made light of your mother."

"Don't apologize—you were being honest. It's not like I can tell you how to live your life. You're the one who has to live with the choices you make, not me."

"Thanks," Cecil mumbled.

"Just know I'm here if you ever wanna chat. Nobody deserves to feel alone."

"How kind of you."

"It's the truth." Aurora picked her nail. "Just promise me you'll at least think about being honest with Roman. I really am not trying to lecture you, but secrets have a way of eating at people. And I don't want to see anything bad happen to you."

"I'll keep that in my mind."

"Crushes don't always have to be a bad thing."

"Excuse me?"

"Don't you remember my crush on Tommy last year?" Aurora asked.

"Yeah, I do."

"He didn't feel the same way, yet he wasn't angry with me. In fact, we even became good friends."

Cecil elevated his eyebrows. "What's your point?"

"That your crush on Roman isn't this disastrous situation you think it is. At the very least, it could strengthen your friendship with Roman."

"I don't know about that."

"I think I'm right about this one."

"If you say so."

Aurora narrowed her gaze. "Are you afraid something will happen to Roman if you get closer to him? Like Scarecrow might hurt him?"

"Scarecrow already tried to harm Roman, although maybe you forgot about that." Cecil exhaled a long breath. "Anyway, I don't mean to be rude, but I've gotta go."

Cecil walked away from Aurora without looking back at her. Certain situations allowed for minor rudeness, and his conversation with Aurora was one of those moments. In an ideal situation, Aurora wouldn't have mentioned his crush on Roman. Yet she had. Therefore, Cecil hoped his subsequent conversations with Aurora wouldn't get more awkward. If he wanted to defeat Scarecrow, then he needed his BFF by his side. And that wouldn't happen if they got distracted by trivial things like school crushes—there'd be time for that later.

***

Cecil and Roman sat at Aurora and Mr. Dexley's dining room table, playing cards. Aurora and Mr. Dexley were in the study enjoying a game of chess, so Cecil and Roman had privacy.

Being thankful for alone time couldn't be helped, though. And Cecil's reasoning wasn't because he felt like confessing his crush to Roman. He just knew it'd be awkward if Aurora hung out with him and Roman. While Cecil didn't doubt Aurora would never intentionally hurt, revelations had a way of being dropped at odd times. And Cecil loathed the idea of Aurora spilling the truth about his feelings towards Roman. He'd protect that secret with his life, so there was no debate to be had about the matter.

Roman beamed. "Thanks again for inviting me over. We should hang out one on one more."

"Yeah, that'd be nice."

Roman coughed into his arm. "I also wanted to thank you again for saving my life. I don't know what I would've done if you hadn't stopped Scarecrow from drowning me."

Cecil's gaze remained on the cards he held. "Don't worry about it. What are friends for, right?"

"True." Roman made a clucking noise with his tongue. "There's something I wanted to mention. I mean, it'd be nice to think we can speak frankly."

"Sure. Go ahead."

"Lena and I were gonna go for ice cream tomorrow after school, and I was wondering how you might feel about that."

"My opinion doesn't matter."

"Don't be silly, Cecil. Your feelings count more than you realize."

"If you wanna spend time with Lena, then you should. But I'm not the one who you should ask. Jace and Lena have practically been dating since kindergarten and I can't imagine he'd be happy knowing you two will be spending alone time together."

"Jace isn't the one I'm concerned about."

"What's that supposed to mean?" Cecil demanded.

"Nothing. Let's just get back to the game."

An empty feeling spread through Cecil's insides while he returned his attention to the cards in his hands. He wanted nothing more than to be honest with Roman. However, he couldn't bring himself to mention how he really felt. The thought of being honest and vulnerable terrified him in light of his orphan status—almost as if Cecil didn't know how to be happy. Besides, Aurora wasn't completely wrong. Cecil wondered what would happen to Roman if he confessed his crush. Like if them being closer meant Scarecrow would give Roman special attention with making his life unbearable. And Cecil couldn't have that. He wouldn't be able to live with himself if something bad happened to Roman.

***

"You should've been honest with your feelings," Aurora said sometime later while swaths of moonlight glinted through the kitchen window while she and Cecil devoured their hot cocoa. "Roman gave you the perfect opening."

Cecil let out a nervous laugh. "I don't know about that."

"You'll never know unless you try."

"It's whatever at this point."

Aurora giggled. "Can't imagine Jace will be thrilled about Roman and Lena hanging out one on one."

"I had the same thought."

"Perhaps you'll change your mind about telling Roman how you feel."

"Doubtful."

Cecil drank more of his rich chocolatey beverage, enjoying the mixture of the chocolate's sweet and bitter flavors. Life would go on even if Cecil didn't tell Roman the truth about his crush. That much Cecil remained certain of.

Upping the Antics

Grey clouds veiled the sky while Cecil, Aurora, Lena, Roman, and Jace stood with their class outside of the Hicklewapper Orchard. Not every field trip proved fun. However, Cecil wouldn't complain about his class visiting what was basically both a farm and an apple orchard. There were worse places to be. As nice as Mr. Hickler acted, Cecil couldn't get over his teacher's monotone voice. So, if a field trip meant taking a break from his teacher droning on and on again, then Cecil welcomed the reprieve. It was nothing personal, truly. Some people just shouldn't have been teachers. And Mr. Hickler was one of those people. In fact, he might've been one of those people who was better fitted for an office job.

"Remember, class," Mr. Hickler said. "The day is yours to do with it as you want, but you've gotta be out here by the orchard's front entrance at one o'clock so we can take the bus back to school. Understand?"

Everyone gave Mr. Hickler a cursory nod while relief washed over Cecil. Since the outing was unstructured, the field trip resembled a day off from school. And Cecil couldn't contain his giddiness. He never once heard of a field trip being a free for all. However, Cecil wouldn't argue with Mr. Hickler. Situations rarely broke in Cecil's favor. Therefore, Cecil would enjoy the win while he could. Doing so was the only logical option for Cecil. It'd be back to the boring school routine in no time. So, Cecil hoped the field trip would go by slowly.

Everyone broke off into their own little cliques while Cecil, Aurora, Lena, Roman, and Jace remained by their current location. If Cecil wanted to be honest with himself, then he needed to admit the excursion not going by too quickly wasn't the only thing on his mind. He prayed Scarecrow wouldn't appear. Cecil couldn't afford Scarecrow doing another terrible thing. The list of Scarecrow's misdeeds got longer with every day that went on, and Cecil wasn't sure how much longer he could keep count. The only situation exhausted Cecil, truly. Mom died. Then Mr. Fickler died. And then Scarecrow tried to burn him to death when Cecil fetched the tissues from the supply closet. Plus, Cecil couldn't forget about Roman almost dying—it'd be a long time before that incident would be erased from his mind. Trying to murder an adult proved bad enough. Yet wanting to harm an innocent kid—like Roman—seemed extra cruel, proving Scarecrow more than crossed the line with his vendetta against Cecil. If Scarecrow wanted to settle a score, then he should've gone after Cecil directly. Doing so would've been the less cowardly thing to do. According to Cecil, that was. He imagined some people might feel differently about the situation. Even if there was no way to spin behaving like a homicidal lunatic.

Roman chuckled. "One of these days you're gonna have to learn not to get distracted by your own thoughts, buddy."

Cecil's jaw quaked. "What?"

Aurora gave Roman a dirty look. "Lay off, Cecil. It's not like you've got any room to talk with the way you've been behaving."

Roman scoffed. "What's that supposed to mean?"

Aurora placed her hands on her hips. "Hanging out with Lena, really?"

"It's a free country," Roman said.

Jace shifted his weight towards Lena. "Is this true?"

Lena waved her hand through the air. "Calm down."

"Please don't suggest I relax," Jace said. "You know I hate it when people tell me to do that. Or has all the time we spent together been a big joke to you?"

"Getting ice cream with Roman wasn't a big deal," Lena said. "You're the one who said you're too young to think about dating. And I thank you for telling me that, because you're right. We can't be expected to know what we wanna do for the rest of your life at thirteen. That's ludicrous. And I'm sure most people would agree with me."

Aurora quirked her eyebrows. "Roman using you both get to Cecil is still wrong, and you know it. Actually, it's disgusting."

Roman snickered. "No need to be melodramatic."

"It's not my fault if you can't accept reality," Aurora said. "Cecil is a kind, decent person who just happens to be going through more than the average person."

Jace snorted. "Ain't that the truth!"

"It's not a joke, Jace," Aurora said. "It could just as easily be you going through a difficult situation. So, you have no reason to judge. Understand?"

"If you say so," Jace replied.

Lena's gaze drifted towards Cecil. "Does me spending time with Roman bother you?"

Cecil didn't blink. "Not at all. You're free to spend time with whoever you want. Just like I'm free to go for a walk in the woods."

Roman gave Cecil a funny look. "Why would you wanna go for a walk in the woods? You could do that any old time. Wouldn't you rather pick apples, go for a hayride, or explore the corn maze?"

Cecil folded his arms. "There's nothing wrong with knowing what I want. At least I don't play games."

"And what's that supposed to mean?" Roman asked.

"Nothing, so don't get so defensive," Cecil said. "I was referring to Scarecrow. I mean, what he's doing is beyond messed up. But that still doesn't change how what he's doing is basically one, sick twisted game."

Lena grinned. "Well put. You should be a writer."

"Maybe I will," Cecil whispered.

Aurora ran her fingers through her hair. "Nothing good is gonna come from you and Lena spending time together. In fact, it's pathetic."

A burning sensation jabbed Cecil's throat. It didn't matter if Aurora was careful when making her comment since she hadn't revealed his crush on Roman. The current conversation made Cecil uncomfortable. And maybe, just maybe, Cecil would ditch his friends so he could clear his head by going for a walk in the woods. Nice idea, anyway. Some truisms contained profound truths despite sounding obvious or simplistic. Nature allowed people to clear their heads. And Cecil needed to seize the opportunity if he wanted to preserve his sanity. No explanation necessary about how his friends talked in circles, which meant their bickering could go on all day. After all, Cecil didn't have time for that. Witnessing the petty squabbles between Aurora and her friend meant Cecil hit his quote for silly disagreements.

"I'm gonna go for a walk," Cecil said. "And please don't follow me."

Aurora bit her lip. "No offense, but you're out of your mind if you think we're gonna let you wander around the orchard alone. Doing so would give the perfect opportunity for Scarecrow to strike. And we can't have that."

"Darn," Cecil said.

Roman scratched the back of his neck. "Aurora's right."

"No surprise there," Aurora touted.

"I still can't believe we're going for a stroll in the woods." Roman tucked his hands into his jacket pockets while tree branches shook in the wind while he, Cecil, Aurora, Jace, and Lena made their way through the woods on the property. "The whole point of this field trip is doing something we wouldn't normally do. So, no disrespect intended or anything, but it kinda sucks how you lack imagination, Cecil."

"Nobody is stopping you if you'd rather do something else," Aurora said. "In fact, maybe you should bring Lena."

"Leave me out of it!" Lena's scarf bounced in the wind. "Getting ice cream with a friend isn't this big deal that everyone keeps making it out to be."

"It meant something to me," Roman said, voice cracking slightly.

"It's time to lighten the mood," someone said.

Cecil's back hairs rose. Unfortunately, he would've recognized that annoying raspy voice anywhere. It belonged to Scarecrow. And Cecil didn't even want to contemplate what bad thing Scarecrow might've planned.

Cecil hissed. "Go away...nobody wants you here!'"

"I beg to differ," Scarecrow said.

Scarecrow snapped his fingers, then a nearby tree rattled violently. One branch grabbed Lena's arm while another grabbed Jace's arm.

"What the heck?" Lena said, stuttering.

Jace pouted. "Let me guess Scarecrow did this?"

"Yup," Cecil said.

"Do your worst." Scarecrow vanished, then the tree resumed shaking. Jace and Lena bobbed out, whimpering.

"We've gotta do something!" Cecil said.

Aurora cracked a small smile. "Good thing I came prepared."

"And what's that supposed to mean?" Roman asked.

Aurora unzipped her backpack and pulled out a mini saw. She dashed over to the tree, cutting the branches holding Jace and Lena captive. In fact, Cecil would've even gone as far as to say Aurora used the same precision and accuracy that a snake would use when striking its prey. And Cecil didn't know whether to be terrified or relieved. On the one hand, Aurora's fast reflexes were handy. Yet on the other hand, Cecil wouldn't want to cross Aurora. No telling what might happen if someone got on her bad side.

Roman's jaw lowered. "You brought a saw?"

"I thought it might come in handy," Aurora said.

"For once, I don't disagree with Aurora," Lena said.

Sweat dripped down Roman's forehead. "You could get in trouble if Mr. Hickler saw you carrying a weapon."

"It's for self-defense," Aurora said.

"Doesn't matter," Roman said.

Jace made eye contact with Aurora. "Thanks for saving Lena and me."

"Don't mention it." Aurora returned the saw to her backpack, then zipped it up.

Lena's lips quivered. "We should get out of here."

"Yeah, I think you're right about that," Cecil said.

Lena's eyebrows knitted together. "You aren't gonna argue with me? I mean, this whole walk in the woods thing was your idea?"

"it's fine," Cecil said.

"What are we waiting for?" Jace asked. "Let's leave."

Jace darted away from Cecil, Aurora, Lena, and Roman. And Cecil didn't blame Jace. They had enough excitement for one day, proving Cecil didn't want to speculate about what antics might happen during the rest of the field trip.

A Big Lie

Cecil and Lena stood on the front porch at Aurora's house while the blue waned from the afternoon sky. Aurora and her father had gone to town to run errands, and that meant Cecil and Lena had the place to themselves. However, Cecil had no idea about why Lena wanted to chat with him. But Cecil wasn't one to turn away a friend. Chatting with Lena also provided a distraction from thinking about Scarecrow, and that was a good thing as far as Cecil was concerned. Scarecrow making the tree come to lie wasn't as bad as beheading Mom or Mr. Fickler, yet violence remained unacceptable. So, Cecil needed to concoct a solution to the Scarecrow situation like yesterday. No telling what dastardly deed Scarecrow might commit tomorrow. Just because Lena and Jace were okay didn't mean Scarecrow's antics at the Hicklewapper Orchard were okay—they weren't.

"You sure you don't want to come inside?" Cecil asked. "I could make you some hot cocoa. And I'm sure I could whip something up from the fridge."

Lena let out a small smile. "That's really sweet of you Cecil, but I can't stay for long. However, that doesn't make what I've gotta say any less important."

"Okay. But you're gonna have to give me a clue about what's on your mind."

"Yeah, I realize we aren't close."

Cecil gaped. He wouldn't have put it as bluntly as Lena. However, she was right. Therefore, Cecil wouldn't argue with her. Doing so would've wasted time he didn't have. And Cecil couldn't afford to be careless with time. Time was a luxury he could never get back once it was gone. So, he needed to make the most of every moment. Or at least try to. Looking back in several decades and being overwhelmed with regret wasn't something Cecil wanted, and he'd do his best not to let that happen.

"I didn't mean anything bad by my comment," Lena continued. "I was only stating a fact. It's not like I have anything against you."

"Good to know."

"I'm serious, Cecil."

Cecil snort laughed. "Just tell me what's on your mind. Who knows. Maybe I'll be able to help you."

"You have it backwards."

"Come again?"

"It's not about what you can do for me. It's about what I can do for you."

Annoyance flickered inside Cecil. Getting a distraction from Scarecrow was one thing. However, Cecil still couldn't stand people who couldn't get to the point. Talking in circles was never a good idea. Life was already complicated enough as it was. And if Lena wanted to have a productive conversation, then Cecil needed her to be clearer and more succinct. It wasn't like Cecil expected any miracles—he didn't.

Cecil just had no desire to talk in ambiguities. Cecil deserved better than that. He also hoped Lena realized she deserved better than that. Friendships were also about being real, so Cecil wouldn't lose sight of that idea. Not anytime soon. His friends were what would get him through this twisted game with Scarecrow.

"I'm still not following," Cecil said.

"The field trip clarified things for me. More specifically, how I can't afford to act foolishly. You know what I'm saying?"

"I'm sorry about Scarecrow targeting you, truly. Any more innocent people being hurt is the last thing I wanted."

"I don't need your apology," Lena said.

"Then what?" Cecil demanded.

"I have no interest in Roman other than friendship. So, you can do whatever you want about your crush."

Cecil must've misheard Lena—she couldn't know about his crush on Roman. That was like saying the sky wasn't blue. So, yeah. There had to be a logical explanation for Lena said moment earlier. Cecil just didn't know what it was.

Cecil avoided Lena's gaze. "Don't be ridiculous...I don't have a thing for Roman."

"No offense, but you're a terrible liar."

"Does everyone know how I feel?" Cecil averted his gaze. "Please don't tell me you've discussed this with Roman?"

"Relax. I know when a situation requires discretion. What do you take me for...some kind of an idiot?"

"You may be a lot of things, but being stupid isn't one of them." Cecil remained silent for a moment. "Why be honest with me about how you feel?"

"Because Roman's plan was foolish."

"What are you talking about?"

"He only wanted to spend time with me to get some sort of reaction out of you."

Cecil crossed his arms. "Why would Roman do something like that? No offense to him, but that sounds childish."

"I'll spell it out for you in case you can't see the truth. Roman feels the same way about you as you do about him."

"How do you know that?"

Lena's face lit up. "He told me so himself."

"This isn't a prank?"

"Do I look like I'm kidding?"

"Good point. But I don't understand why you went along with Roman's plan. The whole thing seems beneath you. Especially since you and Jace have always been so close."

"Jace has been too preoccupied with family and school stuff, so I thought it might be a good idea to shake things up."

"Wow. And I thought my mother was melodramatic."

"It's not like anyone got hurt," Lena said.

"You do know I'm not gonna keep this revelation to myself, right? I'm gonna have to chat with Roman."

"Oh, I'm counting on it."

"Does Roman know you won't be spending anymore one on one time together?"

Lena nodded. "He knows and has accepted it."

Cecil stroked his jaw. "Why couldn't Roman be honest with me about how I felt? His antics seem like something out of a bedtime story."

"I could ask you the same thing."

Cecil appreciated Lena's honesty. However, he despised her turning the situation around on him. Roman's behavior was the current issue, not Cecil's. And that meant Cecil refused to be blamed for something.

"Huh?" Cecil asked.

"You couldn't be honest with Roman either."

"Yeah, that's true."

Lena stared Cecil down. "And I wonder why that is?"

"Even you can't be oblivious to how there's a lot going on."

"True. Anyway, I gotta go but I wish you luck with your situation."

Cecil blinked. "Really?"

"Don't act so surprised. I'm not nearly as heartless as everyone makes me out to be."

"Thanks for your honesty."

"Don't mention."

Lena's bombshell weighed on Cecil's mind while he remained on the front porch and Lena descended the steps. Roman's behavior was beyond childish. However, everyone made mistakes, including Cecil. So, maybe, just maybe, Cecil would need to show Roman some grace. Roman might not have gone about things the right way, yet he clearly cared. And that was something to hold onto.

***

Cecil shuffled towards Roman the following morning at school. Roman just took a sip of water from the water fountain, and Cecil's heart hadn't stopped racing. What Cecil had to say wouldn't be easy, but there was no substitute for the truth. He complained to himself about how Lena wasn't being direct with him the previous day with getting to the point sooner. So, taking his own advice was the least Cecil could do.

Roman chuckled. "Everything okay?"

"Lena told me everything." Cecil drew in a breath. "But I don't even know where to begin. Using Lena to provoke some sort of reaction out of me is beyond childish. However, I also know what it's like to be afraid of your feelings."

"She told you that I've got a crush on you?"

"Basically."

"Wow."

"Going forward, it seems like communication is something we need to work on."

"You don't say," Roman replied. "Wait. You aren't angry."

"I'm tired of wasting time."

Roman tugged at his backpack strap. "Where does this leave us?"

"I don't know. Maybe we could hang out one day after school and grab ice cream in town."

"Sounds nice."

Roman's cheeks turned bright. "Why don't I walk you to homeroom?"

"Were in the same homeroom."

"Doesn't matter. Besides, you might need protection from Scarecrow."

"Good point."

Cecil and Roman walked down the hallway while a warm sensation washed over Cecil. As annoying as Aurora sometimes was, she was also right. His situation with Roman went his way, and Cecil appreciated that. Having one thing go right—even something as trivial as a first crush—comforted Cecil. No explanation necessary about how life could be cruel, and Cecil needed to find whatever joy he could."

***

A morbid look remained plastered on Mr. Dexley's face while he, Aurora, and Cecil sat at the dining room table nibbling on chicken drumsticks and mashed potatoes. Cecil wasn't sure how he was supposed to feel about the uneasy look on Mr. Dexley's face. Aurora's father was probably gonna drop a bombshell—whether Cecil liked it or not. And Cecil just hoped the matter wasn't too serious.

Mr. Dexley sucked in a breath. "I lied to you guys, and I'm really sorry. Being dishonest isn't something I strive for—not ever. However, I did what I thought was best."

"What are you talking about, Dad?" Aurora asked.

"About the night Cecil's mother died," Mr. Dexley said. "More specifically, the other weird events."

Cecil clenched his jaw. "What do you mean?"

"The people weren't getting signs from their deceased loved ones." Mr. Dexley rolled his sleeves up. "They were being visited by their former imaginary friends."

"I don't understand," Aurora mused.

"The point is, that something big might be about to go down in Hicklewapper," Mr. Dexley said.

"Why be honest now?" Cecil asked.

"Because you two deserve to know the truth," Mr. Dexley said.

Aurora sneered. "Guess better late than never."

"Don't take that tone with me!" Mr. Dexley snapped, vein surfacing on his forehead.

"That's the thing, Dad." Aurora made a dramatic pause. "You no longer have the moral high-ground—not after keeping so big from Cecil and me."

Mr. Dexley pursed his lips. "Don't say that!"

"It's not mean if it's true."

"I've done more for you than you'll ever know."

Aurora began rambling while Cecil stared off into space. He needed all of one second to realize he was about to witness another argument between Aurora and her father, yet Cecil didn't have it in him to be angry with Mr. Dexley. In fact, the opposite was true. Other people grappling with disgruntled former imaginary friends showed Cecil wasn't alone. And for that Cecil remained thankful. Being one of the few weirdos got tiresome, after all.

Another Fire

The wind whistled louder and faster, pushing a pile of red, orange, and yellow leaves about while Cecil, Aurora, Roman, Lena, and Jace sat at one of the wooden tables in front of the middle school's main entrance. Cecil didn't know exactly what to make of the leaves already changing colors. On a practical level, Cecil realized fall was well under way. Yet a small part of Cecil wanted to pretend it was still summer. Every day that went by meant it was one day closer to winter, and Cecil wasn't ready for it to be cold enough to see his breath. Not now. Not ever. Any positive attributes about winter tapered off as soon as the holiday's ended. Cecil didn't care about seeming negative. Winter never did much for anyone. So, Cecil would be just fine if there were only three seasons instead of four.

Roman bit his lip. "Can't believe there are others dealing with the return of their imaginary friend besides Cecil."

Lena sniggered. "Guess you aren't as special as you thought you were—no offense or anything, Cecil."

"None taken," Cecil said.

Jace eyed Aurora. "Your father didn't mention anything like else? Like if maybe Scarecrow and the other imaginary friends are gonna unite and do something terrible to the town?"

"No, he didn't," Aurora said.

Lena leaned forward. "Maybe that's a good thing. Perhaps Scarecrow is the only imaginary friend focused on revenge."

Cecil let out a nervous laugh. "We can only hope."

Aurora sneered. "My father should've been honest with Cecil and me from the beginning. Doing so would've been both fair and honorable."

Jace laughed. "Not sure what honor has to do with anything."

"We aren't little kids," Aurora spat, face turning slightly red. "Telling us an occasional harsh truth isn't the end of the world."

"I didn't realize you felt so passionately about this," Roman said.

"Wouldn't you be annoyed if one of your parents lied to you?" Aurora asked.

Roman nodded. "Point taken."

Lena rested her free hand under her chin. "I hate to be a downer, but I wonder what Scarecrow's next move will be."

"Yeah, that'd be nice to know," Cecil said.

Lena's eyes bulged. "Any ideas, Cecil?"

"Nope," Cecil mumbled.

Jace frowned at Lena. "Leave him alone. It's not fault Cecil's fault Scarecrow is furious. Cecil grew up."

"Whatever," Lena said.

"The worst part is we're still no closer to finding a solution to dealing with Scarecrow, in addition to not knowing what his next move will be," Aurora said.

Cecil rolled his eyes. "You're telling me."

Roman patted Cecil's back. "It'll be okay."

"What?" Jace asked. "You aren't gonna call him buddy anymore?"

"Nope," Roman said.

Lena snickered. "Guess your talk with Cecil went better than you could've hoped, which is yet another reason you should be thanking me."

"Don't take this the wrong way, Lena, but please don't act like your God's gift to the world," Roman said.

Jace rubbed his temple. "Roman's right—as much as I hate to admit. Arrogance is never a good look."

"I'm sorry about all the drama over the last few weeks." Cecil fought back the lump in his throat. "I never meant for anyone to be in danger. Hopefully, you aren't too angry with me."

"Don't be silly," Roman said.

"Even I'm not mean enough to blame you for someone else's actions," Lena said.

Cecil glanced in Aurora's direction. "Is it possible your father is holding back more information?"

"What do you mean?" Aurora asked.

Cecil shrugged. "Don't know. Just meant maybe he's working on some sort of plan to save the day."

Aurora rubbed the top of her head. "That'd be nice, but unfortunately, nobody is coming to the save the day. It's just the five of us."

Cecil's stomach cartwheeled from Aurora's comment. He knew Aurora and her father had their fair share of issues, yet he didn't realize just how bad things were between the two of them. Aurora should've had more confidence in her father, yet she didn't. And that point wasn't lost on Cecil.

Roman grimaced. "That's a daunting thought."

Jace cackled. "Didn't know you had such a big vocabulary. But hey. There's a first time for everything."

Sweat coated Cecil's palms. "There's something I haven't been honest with you guys, but I don't think I can dance around the topic anymore."

Aurora furrowed her eyebrows. "And what's that?"

"What if I have to die in order to get rid of Scarecrow?" Cecil asked, voice shaking.

"Why would you say something like that?" Roman asked.

"Scarecrow is tethered to me," Cecil said.

Aurora glared at Cecil. "That doesn't mean you have to die, so please don't even think something that outrageous. In fact, you're better than that."

"Do you think I wanna think about something so morbid?" Cecil asked. "Because I don't. I was only being honest."

"Don't worry," Roman said. "We'll find an option for dealing with Scarecrow that doesn't involve anything bad happening to you. There's gotta be some way to destroy Scarecrow without hurting you."

"I hope so," Cecil mumbled.

"I know so," Roman said.

A silence ensued while Cecil, Roman, Aurora, Jace, and Lena continued sitting at the table. Cecil didn't care if he killed the mood by asking his question. He couldn't run from the matter that haunted his mind since that night Scarecrow visited him in his bedroom. The question was naturally, really. Scarecrow wouldn't be alive without Cecil.

"Between the five of us, we gotta know somebody who knows magic," Roman finally said.

"I'm afraid not," Lena said.

"So, what?" Roman asked. "We're just supposed to let Scarecrow continued with his reign of terror while we stand by and twiddle our thumbs? Because that's pretty stupid if you ask me."

Cecil's heart skipped several beats. Being young—such as thirteen—didn't stop Cecil from appreciating the passion in Roman's voice. More specifically, how Roman got worked up on Cecil's behalf. Cecil loved it, and he hoped to experience that fluttering heart sensation more often. In a perfect world, Cecil would depend only on himself. However, Cecil couldn't run from his emotions. Carrying the entire world on his shoulders exhausted Cecil. And for one fleeting moment, Cecil felt less burdened by Roman making it his mission to want to come up with a solution for the Scarecrow situation.

Rain pattered against the ground, then Cecil glanced up at the sky. Funny how fickle the weather was. When Cecil left for school earlier in the morning, there hadn't been one cloud in the sky. Yet now a nasty gray color saturated the clouds.

"Guess it's better than snow," Cecil said.

Lena stood. "Maybe so. But I don't feel like getting rained on, so let's go inside."

Aurora grabbed her bag. "Point taken."

When Lena was right, she was right. If Cecil and his friends were going to be confused and miserable, then they could at least do it from the comfort of inside the school building. Them being drenched in rain wouldn't help anything, after all. Scarecrow would still exist.

***

Cecil walked into the kitchen while sunlight radiated through the kitchen window. Aurora was already in the kitchen. Her back was towards Cecily—she was listening to the radio. And Cecil wondered what was so important that his best friend couldn't even greet him good morning. Rudeness wasn't something he expected from Aurora. Not now. Not ever. Therefore, Cecil hoped everything was okay with Aurora.

Aurora turned the radio turned the radio off, then sighed after facing Cecil. It wasn't long before Cecil's throat tightened. From the look on Aurora's face, she must've been worried about something. And Cecil wasn't sure he wanted to know what it was. Cecil didn't know what he'd do if Scarecrow did one more bad thing.

Cecil expelled a nervous laugh. "Dare I ask what's wrong?"

"School's cancelled indefinitely."

"Is this a joke?"

"Nope."

"I'm not getting your point, so please be cleared about whatever it is that you're trying to say."

"The middle school burned to the ground last night," Aurora asked.

Cecil gaped. "Wow."

"The town has no idea about who started the fire, but they're vowing to get to the bottom of the situation and hold the guilty person accountable."

"I see."

"I'm just gonna say it if you won't. Scarecrow did this, right?" Aurora asked.

"Probably," Cecil whispered.

"They're just lucky nobody got hurt."

"That's good to hear."

"Yeah, that's about the only good news from the situation."

"If my father doesn't know magic, then maybe he can make an invention that can help us."

"That'd be nice."

Aurora's gaze narrowed. "That's all you've gotta say?"

"What do you want me to say?" Cecil spat.

"Something's clearly on your mind…"

Cecil couldn't make eye contact with Aurora. "I'm worried about my comment from the other morning. What if I have to die in order for Scarecrow to be defeated?"

"Then we'll just find another solution and that's all there is to it." Aurora wrapped an arm around Cecil while relief pulsed through him. Thank goodness Aurora hadn't argued with him mentioning his concern was frivolous. Doing so would've wasted time they didn't have.

There was just no telling what Scarecrow's next move would be, after all.

The Talk

Cecil and Roman stood by the oven while the aroma of warm apples, cinnamon, and sugar wafted through the kitchen. He just couldn't get over the tightness in his chest, though. Somehow, Cecil was spending time with his crush after revealing his true feelings, and the world hadn't ended. Because he would've expected Hicklewapper to implode before ever getting his way with a situation. However, life could occasionally be generous. Therefore, Cecil would take the win—he had to. Cecil needed all of one second to realize it wouldn't be long before he complained about some new unfortunate incident. So, Cecil hoped hanging out with Roman would last forever.

Roman chuckled. "I've never made apple pie before."

"Cool. I'm glad you get to experience this with me."

"Hopefully, it'll turn out okay."

"Duh. Of course, the pie will be fine." Cecil drew in a deep breath. "And if you don't believe me, then believe the oven timer."

"Fair enough." Roman smirked. "No offense or anything, but I never expected you to get so passionate about baking."

"It was something my mother and I used to do."

"I see."

Cecil laughed. "It's okay, Roman. You don't have to act like I'm gonna break on a moment's notice. I don't mind discussing my mother in small doses."

"That's mature of you."

"I don't have a choice," Cecil said. "This apple pie even proves that."

"What does pie have to do with your mother?"

"She made an apple pie the day she died." Cecil coughed, clearing the uneasiness from her voice. "So, either I can associate pie with the day she died. Or I can make a positive new memory about pie."

Roman gasped. "Wow. That's profound."

"You gotta do what you gotta do."

"Very true."

Cecil's breathing slowed down while he maintained eye contact with Roman. He hadn't put on a façade for Roman. Cecil meant what he said about needing to have a new positive association with apple pie. Letting Scarecrow rob him of his love of his sweets would've been idiotic. One bad memory shouldn't have ruined something for the rest of his life, after all. It wasn't like Scarecrow used the apple pie to kill Mom. And for that, Cecil remained thankful. No explanation necessary about how twisted the irony would be if Scarecrow killed Mom with something she intended to be a tasty treat.

"I don't want you to think I'm laying it on thick with what I'm about to say, so please don't take it that way," Roman said.

"Okay..."

"You're a strong person, and I'm proud of how you're handling yourself. Don't think I could be so strong."

Cecil blushed. "There's no need for flattery, but thanks. That means a lot."

"Can't you take a compliment?"

"Guess not."

"Let me guess...it's because you're always in survival mode?"

"You said it, not me."

"I hate how this is your life now, but don't worry. Scarecrow's reign of terror can't last forever. We'll be victorious over Scarecrow—just you wait."

Cecil's face drooped. "I know you're only trying to comfort me, but please don't make promises you can't keep. There's no telling what might happen because of this Scarecrow situation."

"Wouldn't you rather have false hope than no hope?"

"That's not the point."

"Then what is?"

"We're dealing with a difficult situation, and coming up with a solution won't be easy. That's just all there is to it."

Roman's cheeks turned pale. "I just hope you sacrifice yourself and let yourself die in hopes of defeating Scarecrow."

"Don't put words in my mouth!" Cecil quipped.

"I can't help it. Some bells can't be un-rung."

"Let me ask you something. You wouldn't worry about possibly having to die to defeat Scarecrow if you were me?"

Roman's jaw trembled. "Okay. Fine. You might have a point. However, worrying isn't gonna get you anywhere."

"Mind if we change the subject?"

"Sure. What's up?"

"I'm just glad we were able to be honest with each other. I know it wasn't easy, but we got to an honest place eventually."

"Same."

Cecil winked. "That's all you've gotta say?"

"What do you want me to say?"

The oven chimed. Cecil grabbed the oven mitts and placed them on his hands in a matter of seconds, then he removed the pie from the oven and put it on the stove. Glee soon radiated from Roman's face, which meant only one thing. Cecil had to burst Roman's bubble. They'd have to wait a little while before having pie because they needed to let it cool off. And Cecil knew Roman well enough that he might be annoyed by that.

Cecil wagged a finger. "Don't get any ideas about having some pie. At least not yet, anyway."

"What? Gonna make me eat my vegetables before I have pie?"

Perhaps Roman had a future as a comedian. Joking about being forced to eat vegetables wasn't something that would've occurred to Cecil, proving humor was Roman's strength, not Cecil's. And that was why. Life would've been boring if everyone shared the same interests. And that wouldn't be good. Cecil hated boredom almost as much as he despised Scarecrow.

Cecil snickered. "No, silly. We have to let it cool off."

"Whatever..."

"I'm serious, Roman!"

"If that's what you want, then that's what we'll do."

"And you better believe it."

Roman folded his arms. "When did you get so strict?"

"I'm not being harsh. I'm just being realistic."

"Okay, then..."

"Let me guess. You're just teasing me?"

"Yup."

"Well played, Roman."

"Thanks, I think. But seriously. We better have some pie soon."

Cecil nudged Roman. "You need to learn some patience. But that'd be like hoping for pigs to fly."

"Anyway, I owe you an apology." Roman gave Cecil a pleading look. "Using Lena to get a rise out of you by making you jealous was wrong of me. And I'll never do something so foolish again. Hopefully, you won't resent me for that forever."

"Nobody's perfect."

Roman clapped Cecil's shoulder. "Thanks."

Cecil hadn't humored Roman by wanting to move beyond Roman's childish behavior. Holding onto past anger and disappointment wouldn't do Cecil any good. It wasn't like bitterness could be traded for gold. No, that wasn't something that ever happened. Not even in the tales Cecil used to read before bed.

"Jace must be relieved about how you're no longer spending quality time with Lena," Cecil finally said.

"Yeah, I agree."

Cecil smirked. "Let's have some pie!"

"We don't have to wait longer?"

"No, we've waited long enough."

Cecil grabbed two plates from the cabinets, and then grabbed the pastry knife from one of the kitchen drawers. Since Roman was Cecil's guest, he'd cut Roman's slice first. Doing so was the polite thing to do. Mom being dead didn't mean Cecil forgot every value she instilled him over the years. That being said, Cecil hoped Roman would enjoy the pie. Cecil was a lot of things, but he wasn't his mother. No explanation necessary how her apple pie was probably better than his.

***

Cecil's locker snicked after he closed it once he stuffed his backpack with everything he needed for his morning classes. Someone tapped Cecil's back. He spun around, offering Aurora a brief smile.

Aurora locked her fingers together. "Glad I caught you, because we need to chat."

"Did I do something wrong?"

"Not at all."

"Then what's up?"

"I want you to be careful with Roman."

"What do you mean?" Cecil asked.

"Yeah, it's great he also has a crush on you. However, I haven't forgotten about his childish antics with using Lena to get under your skin."

"I see."

"Tell me you haven't forgotten about that?"

"No, I haven't."

"Okay. Good."

Cecil nibbled on the inside of his lip. "I appreciate you looking out for me, but I'm not a little kid."

"Never said you were."

"Maybe I should turn the tables on you."

"Huh?"

Cecil chuckled. "You've been awfully quiet about your life. And for all I know, you could be crushing on a new guy."

Aurora looked away from Cecil. "Don't be ridiculous!"

"Whatever you say."

"Hopefully, you understand my concern about you and Roman is just about being a good friend and looking out for you. I'm not trying to be mean...I swear it."

"Relax, I believe it."

Cecil hadn't told Aurora what she wanted to hear to appease her. There were worse things in the world than having an overprotective friend. It wasn't lost on Cecil how some people wandered through life alone. Like Scarecrow, for example. Cecil couldn't wrap his head around what it'd be like to be someone else's imaginary friend.

***

Cecil woke up, almost screaming. He had another nightmare about Scarecrow beheading Mom. And Cecil wanted to put about a million miles between himself and the dream. He could only relieve Mom's death so many times. Nobody deserved to deal with so much trauma. Except maybe Scarecrow, but that was beside the point.

"Bad dream?" Scarecrow asked.

Goosebumps formed on Cecil's back, arms, and legs. Scarecrow invading his privacy by entering his bedroom would never be okay with Cecil, and Cecil looked forward to the day when he never had to witness another uninvited accosting from Scarecrow again. Only then would Cecil finally be at peace.

"You could at least answer my question," Scarecrow continued.

"I don't owe you anything."

"Have it your way." Scarecrow screeched. "Just came to warn you about Hicklewapper Founder's Day celebration in town."

"What are you getting at?"

"Something's big gonna go down, but you won't know what it is. Because knowing your hero complex, you and your friends won't be able to stay away from the festivities."

"Burning down the middle school wasn't enough for you?"

"I was wondering when you were gonna mention that."

"How could you torch my school? Someone could've been killed."

"But they weren't.

"Are other imaginary friends involved in your plan?"

Scarecrow cackled. "What do you mean? I'm a one-man operation."

Cecil's lips curled. "Aurora's father mentioned something about other people he knew getting visits from their imaginary friends."

"Yeah, that's true. But I'm the only one who wants revenge?"

Cecil blinked, almost choking. "Really?"

"Guess the others don't have the stomach for revenge."

"See. It pays to have a conscience."

"Not really—the others are just weak."

"Whatever you say."

"Bye." Scarecrow waved at Cecil, then vanished.

A scorching sensation once again jabbed Scarecrow's stomach. Being annoying didn't mean Scarecrow was never right. In this case, Scarecrow's assessment was correct. Knowing something terrible was going to go down at the upcoming town festivities meant Cecil wouldn't be able to stay away from the Founder's Day celebration. Even if that meant putting himself in danger. Cecil just couldn't let any more innocent be shed. It was a promise.

A Plea for Help

Wind slammed against the house while Cecil stood in the kitchen. Aurora was at ballet practice and Mr. Dexley was running an errand in town, so Cecil had the house to himself. He didn't know whether to be pleased with having the freedom or if he should be terrified from how Scarecrow might strike at any moment. Scarecrow's warning about the upcoming Founder's Day celebrations wasn't something Cecil would forget anytime soon. The only problem was Cecil didn't know what Scarecrow was planning. His former imaginary friend seemed to have a thing for fire. So, Cecil could see Scarecrow setting all of downtown Hicklewapper on fire. Yet torching a place wasn't the only way to harm people. Therefore, there was no telling what sinister thoughts might've been swirling in Scarecrow's mind.

Cecil snatched the flier from the kitchen counter, sighing. The Founder's Day celebrations were supposed to be a happy time. Not something that inspired constant fear. Because the dread was palpable.

And Cecil was running out of time to come up with a solution for dealing with Scarecrow.

Blaming anyone else for the predicament was foolish, though. Cecil only had himself to blame for how he hadn't contained Scarecrow. Except permanently erasing Scarecrow from existence wasn't quite a walk in the park. And without anything short of a miracle, Cecil was doomed.

The outside wind roared louder while the pattering of rain echoed. One night when he was eight shouldn't have impacted his life so much. Yet that fateful night had. And Cecil would've given anything to turn back time and stop Scarecrow from being created. Then Mom and Mr. Fickler would still be alive...

***

Cecil sat in his bedroom crying shortly after his eighth birthday. Mom was outside gardening, so Cecil didn't have to worry about his mother witnessing his emotional moment and having to deal with the subsequent embarrassment of Mom discovering his sobbing. No explanation necessary about how seeming pathetic was never ideal—whether someone was eight or eighty-eight.

However, if Cecil wanted to be honest with himself, then he needed to admit he shouldn't have even been worried about Mom eavesdropping on his emotional moment. Digging deeper and being completely honest meant acknowledging how Mom hadn't been helpful since Dad died. They hadn't even discussed Dad's death once. In fact, they hadn't even had a funeral for Dad. And to say that surprised Cecil would've been an understatement. Even little kids usually understood how funerals happened when people died.

But no. Mom hadn't wanted a funeral. Something about how having a memorial would've been too morbid and how holding onto the positive memories was the best option. Almost as if Mom couldn't admit Dad was absolutely, positively dead.

Cecil's wailing echoed through his bedroom, tears dripping onto the ground. Then, a mist formed. A scarecrow stood in the mist's place once the mist was gone.

"What's going on?" Cecil asked.

Scarecrow beamed. "I'm your imaginary friend, and I'll always be here for you—don't you forget it.".

Cecil choked. "Really?"

"Absolutely."

Surprise fizzled inside Cecil. He never expected something as strange as an imaginary friend forming from his tears, but Cecil wouldn't argue when something favorable happened. No explanation necessary about how Cecil couldn't be certain when the next good thing might happen to him. Unfortunately for Cecil, misfortunate had a way of following him. And Cecil would've given just about anything to change his luck. He wasn't asking for the moon and the stars. He only wanted to believe happiness and goodness was possible again. For all intents and purposes, it was like ice replaced Cecil's heart after Dad died. He just didn't know how to go about living his life again.

Scarecrow chuckled. "You don't talk much, do you?"

"Can't help it. I have a lot on my mind."

"Understood."

Cecil gritted his teeth. "In case you didn't know it, my dad recently died. And I have no idea how I'm supposed to live the rest of my life."

"Sorry to hear that. But have no fear. I'll always be here for you through the good times and bad times. And the best part of all is how you'll be the only one who can hear and see me. So, you never have to worry about someone ruining our connection."

Cecil blinked. "This can't be real?"

"Oh, but it is."

***

A clap of thunder snapped Cecil out of his digression. Despite Scarecrow being born a little over five years ago, he remembered the day like it was yesterday. And it didn't matter how much time went by. For better or for worse, Cecil would always recall every moment of his first conversation with Scarecrow.

Cecil shuddered. To the best of his knowledge, time travel didn't exist. Therefore, Cecil hated living with how Scarecrow came to life because of him. Even if Cecil never intended for everything to go amiss.

A solution had to exist about dealing with Cecil, and he'd discover it if doing so was the last thing he ever did. And no. Cecil wasn't being melodramatic or quirky. He was being serious. With the right amount of determination, anything was possible. Cecil wouldn't have it any other way, though. His tenacity was what would get him through his current debacle. He just knew it. Mom would have never told him to give up, after all. Cecil hoped so, at least.

Cecil crumbled the flier, then threw it across the kitchen. Scarecrow's "birth" wasn't the only moment related to Scarecrow he'd never forget. Another episode from their past stood out for Cecil. And perhaps if Cecil handled the situation better, then Scarecrow wouldn't have concocted this whacky revenge situation—Scarecrow's vendetta against him was truly the most bizarre thing Cecil ever witnessed. An imaginary friend existed to fill the gap during a difficult period of Cecil's life, not to make his life unbearable...

***

A silence ensued while Cecil and Scarecrow stood in Cecil's bedroom a few days after Cecil turned twelve. The dread lingering in the air from the news Cecil just dropped was more than Cecil could happen. He wondered if he made a big mistake. At the very least, Cecil realized he could've been more delicate with how he broke the news to Scarecrow.

Scarecrow pouted. "I can't believe you're ditching me!"

"It's not like I have a choice. You believe me, right?"

"It doesn't matter if I believe you, because your mother is the real problem."

A metallic taste filled Cecil's mouth. Apparently, he bit his lip too hard. And he was going to have work on his nervous tics at some point in the future when he had more free time. For the moment, Scarecrow needed to be the priority. Even if that meant Cecil might look like a nervous wreck from trying to convince Scarecrow that this wasn't how he wanted the situation to unfold in addition to how certain things were out of his control.

"You can't cast me aside like I'm nothing," Scarecrow continued.

"Do you want my mother to send me away?"

"Doesn't sound like she's a very good mother if she's this bothered by you having an imaginary friend. It's not like I'm hurting anyone."

"I know. I know."

"There's gotta be something we can do," Scarecrow said, desperation obvious to Cecil. "This can't be the end of our friendship.

"I'm afraid it is."

"You're gonna regret this one day…just you wait."

***

The outside rain and wind intensified while Cecil cradled his hands behind his head. In a way, Scarecrow was right. And Cecil hated that Scarecrow had the last laugh. Cecil having to grow up didn't justify Scarecrow's childish antics. Nothing excused cold-blooded murder such as what Cecil witnessed when Scarecrow killed Mom and Mr. Fickler.

***

Cecil descended the staircase, heading towards the basement. Aurora's father hadn't been much help yet, so some people might think Cecil was foolish for what he was about to do. However, Cecil needed to shove his doubt aside. His mother's favorite cliché saying about desperate times calling desperate measures was true.

"Are you down here, Mr. Dexley?" Cecil asked.

"Yeah, I'm over here."

Cecil navigated his way through the various clutter in the basement, being careful not to trip over or bump into anything. Then, he took a deep breath once he approached Mr. Dexley, who stood by his work bench.

Mr. Dexley put the wrench down, then looked up Cecil. "What can I do for you?"

"I apologize for sounding pathetic," Cecil said. "But I don't have a choice. I have no other options for dealing with Scarecrow."

"I see."

Increased desperation colored Cecil's face. "Please tell me you have a plan to help me defeat Scarecrow, because right now I'd pretty much accept almost any kind of help. You've got no idea just how bad things go."

"As luck would have it, I'm working on something."

"Really?"

"Yup. However, I didn't wanna say anything because I didn't wanna get your hopes up." Mr. Dexley gave Cecil a weak smile. "The device should be done within the next several days."

"That's good...we don't have much time."

"Is there something specific you know that I don't?"

Cecil nodded.

"Don't be bashful!" Mr. Dexley said. "By all means share."

"I don't know what it is, but Scarecrow is planning something big for the upcoming Founder's Day festivities in a few days."

"Oh dear..."

"My thoughts exactly." Cecil wiped a bead of sweat from his forehead with one flick of his wrist. "Anyway, why don't you tell me about this device."

"Gladly."

Relief slowly trickled through Cecil while he listened to Aurora's father drone on about the device he built. Nothing was guaranteed in life. However, Mr. Dexley's contraption was the best option for defeating Scarecrow. In fact, it was Cecil's only option.

CONFRONTATION

"I can't believe Aurora's father was secretly helping us all along," Roman said while he sat next to Cecil on the park bench while Aurora, Lena, and Jace stood in front of them. They decided to grab ice cream. Cecil needed something calm his nerves if he was going to tell them about Mr. Dexley's plan.

Aurora heaved a sigh. "Guess I should've had more faith in my father. Although I still stand by one of my earlier ideas. Dad should learn to be a better communicator. I mean, I don't have to be a grownup to realize good communication is an important life school."

Lena's lips quivered. "I just hope you know what to do, Cecil. No offense or anything, but the fate of Hicklewapper is in your hands."

Jace gave Lena a funny look. "That's a little dramatic, don't you think?"

"If Scarecrow intends on doing something dastardly at the Founder's Day events, then that means everyone in Hicklewapper is involved even if people don't realize they are," Lena said.

Aurora rolled her eyes. "How eloquently put."

"Now isn't the time for attitude, Aurora." Lena shifted her weight. "Even you can be that oblivious to realize something important is about to go down."

"Exactly," Aurora said. "And that's why we should be encouraging Cecil—not putting doubt in his head."

Roman took another bite of ice cream. "I still don't understand why you have to be the one to use this device."

"I'm the only one who can see Scarecrow...or did you forget about that?" Cecil asked, trying to hide his annoyance.

"Oh, okay. Makes sense." Roman tossed his spoon and empty bowl into an adjacent garbage. "But I still wish you didn't have to do this alone."

"We've already been through this," Cecil said. "I can't risk you, Aurora, Lena, or Jace getting hurt."

"You really think this device will be enough?" Lena asked.

Aurora didn't even wince. "It has to be."

Jace shuddered. "I'm just glad you know what you're doing, because this whole thing is a bit too much."

"It's simple," Cecil said. "Pressing a button on the device will create a portal to the Land of Forgotten Things AKA the afterlife, and that's where I'll zap Scarecrow too."

Any icy sensation washed over Cecil. Discussing death was something kids shouldn't do, yet here they were, going over the plan to defeat Scarecrow once and for all. And Cecil didn't know what to make of that. In theory, dying wasn't something he should think about for a long time—no explanation necessary about how his current age meant he had a long life ahead of him. However, Cecil had more experience with death than he cared to admit. Like how he stared at his bedroom ceiling when it was way past his bedtime, contemplating how he hoped his parents were okay. The Land of Forgotten Things wasn't the same as being alive. But maybe, just maybe, his parents discovered a new normal when adjusting to the afterlife. They had to. Wanting them to find peace was only natural for Cecil.

"But this isn't this only a temporary solution?" Jace finally asked.

"What do you mean?" Cecil demanded.

"What if he finds a way to drop the veil between our world and the Land of Forgotten Things?" Jace asked. "I'm not trying to be critical, but we've gotta be prepared for anything when dealing with Cecil."

Aurora's nostrils flared. "That's not gonna happen. My father might be a lot of things, but he's good at what he does."

"Then why doesn't he have inventions or scientific discoveries to his name...not counting this device he concocted, that is," Lena said.

"You can't rush science," Aurora said.

Lena snorted. "That's a load of nonsense, and even you should know better than to believe I'd buy that garbage."

Cecil sighed. "Let's not fight, guys!"

"It's not a big deal if we hide in the bushes or behind a tree or something," Roman said. "Logically speaking, you're gonna need backup."

"Like I said, it's too dangerous," Cecil said, looking Roman square in the eye. "But I appreciate the gesture."

Snow flurries fell from the sky, and Cecil muttered bad language under his breath. In all his years, Cecil never recalled it snowing so early before. And Cecil wasn't sure if he should be happy or annoyed by the unexpected snow. On the one hand, the weather provided a distraction from thinking about the Scarecrow situation. On the other hand, they just had ice cream, which wasn't something that went with colder weather.

Roman sniggered. "Let me guess. You're annoyed about the dusting of snow we're getting?"

"You bet," Cecil said.

***

Cecil hummed while he made his way through the woods in back of Aurora's house. Maybe, just maybe, Scarecrow would be gullible enough to take the bait—he had to. This plan was the only thing Cecil had, which even resembled a chance of defeating Scarecrow. And that meant failure wasn't an option. The thought of everyone in Hicklewapper suffering some ghastly fate because of Scarecrow still terrified Cecil. Scarecrow was Cecil's problem to deal with, not theirs. So, nobody else could die besides Mom and Mr. Fickler, they just couldn't.

"Come out, come out, wherever you are, Scarecrow," Cecil said. "I'm ready to let you back into my life. If you agree not to harm anyone at the Founder's Day events, that is. I mean, that's a pretty fair deal if you ask me."

Someone squealed. "Did someone say my name?"

Cecil feigned a genuine look. "You came?"

"Of course I came. I'd never ignore you."

"Good to know we're still tethered to each other even if we aren't as close as we once were."

"Don't you realize, silly? We're linked together forever."

"Apparently."

"Anyway, you'd really let me back into your life for good?"

"You've gotta promise not to harm anyone else, though. Do you think you can do that? Or would that be too much for you?"

"Seems reasonable enough to me."

"Good. Anyway, I hope you enjoy your trip to The Land of Forgotten Things—perhaps you can apologize to Mom and Mr. Fickler when you see them." In one swift motion, Cecil whipped out the box from his inside jacket pocket. Then, he pressed a button. Cecil aimed the box towards Scarecrow, and a portal appeared. The end part of the portal pulled Scarecrow—like two magnets being drawn together.

Scarecrow managed to hold onto a nearby tree, though, proving defeating his nemesis might challenge Cecil more than he realized.

Scarecrow screamed. "N-o-o-o!"

"Actions have consequences including yours."

"You can't do this."

"But I am."

"You aren't gonna get away with this."

"Looks like I already did," Cecil touted.

"You're gonna regret this...just you wait."

"I'm so scared," Cecil said in a mocking tone.

Scarecrow hands fell from the tree, and the portal sucked him in. The portal completely disappeared. After that, Cecil tucked the box back inside his jacket pocket.

Cecil cried tears of joy while reveling in his accomplishment. Scarecrow was gone, and this was the best news Cecil heard in a long time. So, Cecil needed to do something to celebrate this victory. He earned it, after all. Because for a moment, Cecil thought he couldn't stop Scarecrow from unleashing his fury on the citizens of Hicklewapper. But no. For once, both time and luck were on Cecil's side.

Being a constant worrier meant Cecil couldn't ignore his rising back hairs while he exited the woods, though. He knew Jace hadn't meant anything bad by the comment, yet Cecil hoped he wouldn't come to eat Jace's words about Scarecrow finding a way to escape The Land of Forgotten Things. This encounter had to be the last time Cecil saw Scarecrow—it had to be. This was one life moment that didn't require a sequel.

Begin Again

Fog cloaked the air while crunching noises echoed from the leaves under Cecil's shoes as he got deeper and deeper into the woods behind the house he once shared with Mom. He didn't care about the idea seeming morbid. For some reason, Cecil wanted to return to the spot in the woods where he, Mr. Dexley, and Aurora buried Mom. Almost as if Cecil wanted closure. Nothing wrong with wanting to close one chapter of his life, after all. Scarecrow was gone, and that was the way things needed to stay. No explanation necessary about how nothing good would come from Scarecrow's return.

Cecil shook his head while he resumed walking. Blaming the victim was usually not a good idea, yet a small part of Cecil still wondered what life would have been like if Mom never made him give up Scarecrow. Then, all this drama could've been avoided. Mainly, Mom would've still been alive.

A certain irony also existed despite Cecil's annoyance from having to give up Scarecrow. Scarecrow turned out to be trouble, just not in the way Mom realized. And Cecil almost laughed at that realization. Cecil could never get over how humor could be found in even the most awkward situations. In theory, nothing about the Scarecrow debacle should've amused Cecil. However, emotions couldn't be suppressed all the time. Not entirely, at least. Doing so was both unrealistic and unhealthy.

Cecil stopped walking once he arrived at the exact spot where he, Aurora, and Mr. Dexley buried Mom. He coughed into his right arm, clearing the scratchiness from his throat. If he wanted to speak to Mom, then he needed to make sure to speak clearly. This wasn't something he could mess up. Cecil had committed enough blunders as it was. And Cecil looked forward to the day when life ran more smoothly.

"I don't know if you can see me from wherever you are in the Land of Forgotten Things," Cecil said. "But I had to come talk to you. I just wanted to let you know I defeated Scarecrow. I mean, I'd like to think you'd be proud of me." He paused for a moment, taking in a deep breath. "I also wanted to apologize. I never meant for any of this to happen. You and Mr. Fickler getting hurt wasn't something I ever wanted. Not ever. But what's done is done. I can't go back and make better choices. The only thing I can do is to live my life with compassion and empathy. And if you see Dad, please tell him I say hello. Because boy do I miss him. Scratch that. I miss both of you."

A twig snapped.

Cecil whirled around, almost tripping when he made eye contact with the person standing in front of him. Luckily for Cecil, though, he wouldn't need to send the person nearby him through a portal to the afterlife. If anyone was going to interrupt Cecil visiting Mom, then it might as well be Roman.

"Aurora said you'd be here," Roman said.

"I see."

"You should've told me you wanted to pay your respects to your mother…I would've come with you."

"That's sweet. But this was something I had to do alone. It's nothing personal, truly. Hopefully, you understand that?"

"I do."

"Good." Roman shoved his hands into his jacket pockets. "Anyway, are you sure you're okay? I mean, besides the obvious with how nobody our age should go through what you've gone through the last few weeks."

"Yeah, I'm fine. Why do you ask?"

"I heard your speech. More specifically, the part about you apologizing." Roman's jaw trembled. "Maybe you realize this, maybe you don't. But guilt won't accomplish anything. One way or another we've gotta move forward."

"I know. I know."

Roman winked. "Anyway, there's something I'd like to do. If you trust me, that is?"

"Of course."

Roman walked over towards Cecil, then gave Cecil a quick peck on the lips. The kiss was over before it even had a chance to begin, but Cecil's pulse wouldn't stop soaring slightly. Something different existed about Roman's kiss than when say his parents would give him a quick kiss on the head when he was a little boy. And Cecil looked forward to spending more time with Roman—that much he knew. They had a special bond, so Cecil would cherish their dynamic as long as he could.

"Was that okay?" Roman asked.

"It was fine."

"Cool. Glad to hear it." Roman blushed. "How about we walk to town and get some ice cream. My treat?"

"That'd be great."

Roman took Cecil's hand and they walked through the woods. In fact, Cecil didn't even give much thought to a nearby owl glaring at him. No, worrying about wild animals could wait till later. Roman's kiss was Cecil's first kiss ever. And Cecil practically squealed with how he got a reprieve with how the kiss hadn't been more awkward.

***

Cecil, Roman, Aurora, Jace, and Lena remained huddled by Cecil's new locker. Scarecrow might've burned down the middle school. However, the mayor and other authority figures decided to reopen the building they were currently in, which had been previously used as the town's middle school up until a few years ago. That was the thing about fun. It didn't last forever. And Cecil couldn't be surprised that he and his friends resumed the school grind.

"Thank goodness Scarecrow is gone," Lena said.

Aurora nodded. "Agreed."

Jace gave Cecil a quick pat on the shoulder. "That was brave of you to deal with Scarecrow by yourself."

"I for one am looking forward to the remainder of the school year being boring," Roman said. "Sometimes, mystery and drama are overrated."

"You could say that again," Lena said.

Cecil swallowed the lump in his throat. "Didn't think I had it in me, but I did it."

"Don't sell yourself short," Aurora said.

Roman grinned. "Definitely agree with Aurora about that one."

Lena rubbed the side of her head. "Darn. I just realized it's a long time between now and the end of the school."

"What are you implying?" Roman asked.

Lena looked at the tile floor. "A lot could happen between now and the last day of school."

"Let's not even put that idea out there," Aurora said.

Lena gave Aurora a small smile. "Fine. Maybe you're right about that."

Footsteps echoed, growing louder with each passing second. Cecil, Roman, Aurora, Jace, and Lena tilted their heads at the same time. A boy several inches taller than Cecil approached Cecil and his friends. The awkwardness of someone they didn't know approaching him and his friends wasn't what bothered Cecil. No, it was the guy's long-sleeved plaid shirt and denim overalls, which was the reason for the knot in Cecil's stomach. Almost as if Cecil had seen this boy before.

"Can we help you with something?" Lena asked.

Aurora nudged Lena. "Don't be rude."

The boy gave them a toothy smile. "I just moved to Hicklewapper...today's actually my first day here at the middle school. The name's Syd. Syd Crow."

Lena giggled. "Like we care."

Syd made eye contact with Cecil. "Don't take this the wrong way, but have we met before? No offense or anything, but I'm getting this strong feeling of déjà vu, and I usually tend to be right about these things."

"And he's arrogant too," Lena murmured.

"I don't think we've met before," Cecil said, fighting back a stutter.

"Oh well. Guess you just have one of those faces." Syd smacked his shoulder against Cecil's. "Guess I'll see you around sometime."

Syd darted down the hallway and was soon out of sight.

The issue of the new boy lingered in Cecil's mind. More specifically, the boy's outfit. And Cecil couldn't forget the name. Syd Crow sounded a lot like Scare Crow.

No, it couldn't be. Cecil trapped Scarecrow in the Land of Forgotten Things. Yeah, the new boy wearing the same outfit that Scarecrow wore had to be a coincidence—it just had to be. Stranger things happened all the time, though. Cecil never once would've guessed his former imaginary friend would turn evil, yet Scarecrow had.

"Something's obviously wrong, Cecil, so spill it," Aurora said.

An icy feeling rolled up Cecil's back. "I don't know how to explain it, but I think Syd is really Scarecrow. Somehow, Scarecrow got reincarnated as a boy. I mean, Syd's sporting the same outfit Scarecrow did. 'Syd Crow' also sounds a lot like 'Scarecrow.' And I really hope you guys don't think I'm crazy."

Aurora rubbed her bottom lip. "It makes more sense than I'd like to admit."

The five of them exchanged glances with each other while more students flocked down the hallway. That was the thing Cecil never liked about life. When one problem ended, another began. And if this new kid really was Scarecrow reincarnated, then Cecil didn't have the faintest clue about what he'd do.

Acknowledgments

I'd like to dedicate this book to all horror fans out there.

About the Author

Chris Bedell is the author of more than a dozen books. He also graduated with a BA in Creative Writing from Fairleigh Dickinson University in 2016.